SECOND TIME AROUND

Amanda reached over and touched Drew's cheek. "I can't believe you actually thought I'd turn you away," she murmured. "I've been in love with you since I was sixteen years old."

The words had barely left her mouth before he pulled her onto his lap and into his arms. His mouth came down on hers just seconds after she recognized the desire blazing in his eyes. She reached up, twining her arms around his neck and leaning into the hard muscles of his chest.

"I want another chance, Amanda. I want to show you just how spectacular it can be." Drew whispered in her ear.

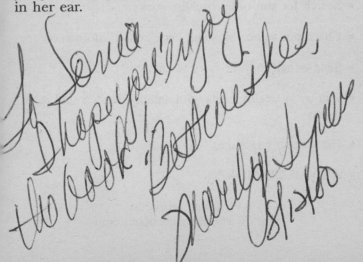

SECRETS OF THE HEART

Marilyn Tyner

BET Publications, LLC
www.msbet.com
www.arabesquebooks.com

ARABESQUE BOOKS are published by

BET Publications, LLC
c/o BET BOOKS
One BET Plaza
1900 W Place NE
Washington, D.C. 20018-1211

First Printing: May, 2000
10 9 8 7 6 5 4 3 2 1

Printed in the United States of America

ACKNOWLEDGMENTS

There are a few people whom I neglected to mention in my previous acknowledgments. First, my children, Cassandra and Robert Tyner. They have both been very enthusiastic and supportive.

Next, Rosa Loper, who has always given me encouragement, while helping me keep my feet on the ground. She has been there for me for many years, in good times and bad. I have been fortunate to find in her that rare commodity, a true friend.

Another person to whom I owe a debt of gratitude is Ardell Thompson, who not only encouraged me to submit my first novel for publication, but graciously agreed to read and critique my first two novels. She also suggested the name of a publisher.

That brings me to the next person on my list, Letitia Peoples, former editor at Odyssey Publishing Co. When she realized her company was financially unable to publish my first novel, she forwarded it to Monica Harris at Kensington. That generous and gracious gesture on her part gave me my start.

Finally, but certainly not least, my cousins, Robert and Beverly Montague, who have attended every one of my booksignings in the area where they live. Not only have they attended the booksignings, but they've come with purchase lists of friends and relatives.

Prologue

Amanda pulled into the restaurant parking lot. After driving up and down the rows a few times, she found a space. Instead of getting out of the car immediately, she sat for a moment with the motor running. But she resisted the temptation to drive away and leave her friend waiting for her inside the restaurant.

Nicole had insisted they celebrate the last of their final exams. Amanda had only agreed because she knew it would be a while before she saw her friend again. She had to be careful not to arouse her friend's suspicions. If Nicole knew what she was planning, she would bombard her with questions. She might even convince her to change her plans.

Amanda looked around as she entered the restaurant. She caught a glimpse of Nicole just as the hostess approached to seat her. Nicole looked up as Amanda made her way through the crowd of tables.

"Hi, girlfriend. How'd it go?"

Amanda shrugged. "Okay, I guess."

"With your 3.8 average, the day you do just 'okay' on an exam, the rest of us are in deep trouble. If the instructors graded on a curve, I wouldn't want to be in any of your classes."

"Thanks for the vote of confidence. You're really good for my morale, Nicole."

Amanda managed to maintain her usual demeanor during the meal. She felt guilty discussing plans for the summer and the fall term when she wouldn't be around for them. When her friend inquired about the courses she would be taking in the fall, Amanda told herself she was being truthful. She had registered for the courses she named. It was just that she would be taking those courses at a different college.

The two parted after lunch. Amanda watched with a lump in her throat as her friend drove away.

When she reached home after her lunch with Nicole, Amanda quickly gathered up her personal belongings. She packed them, rather haphazardly, in the boxes she had collected and stashed away during the past few weeks.

Returning to the house to retrieve the last suitcase, Amanda slowly looked around the bedroom. She was torn between trying to imprint the image indelibly in her mind and hoping she would be able to banish it forever. Some people might think her crazy to be leaving a comfortable home and a man who had always been good to her, even though he was not in love with her.

That was her main reason for leaving. Drew had never been in love with her, and had never pretended to be. She would be able to accept that state of affairs except for the fact that she was deeply in love with him. Her feelings could no longer be considered a teenage infatuation. If she stayed, Drew would soon realize the depth of her feelings, and that discovery would only increase his pity for her.

She wondered if the guilt would ever ease. Guilt over the deception that had started weeks earlier, when she registered for fall classes at a college in neighboring Delaware County. It had been surprisingly easy to rent an apartment in a small town near the college.

A week earlier, she had filed a few applications for employment, using her new address, hoping her lack of work experience would not hinder her. The only job she had held was in Drew's father's office. Under the circumstances, she could hardly expect a glowing reference.

She had to consider the fact that should her new employer contact Drew's office, it would alert him to her whereabouts. Not that she expected him to come running after her. If he contacted her at all, it would probably only be to question her about the money.

At first, Amanda had worried that he would discover the account had been closed, but Drew seldom questioned her activities. He trusted her. That made carrying out her plans much easier. It also made the guilt rise to the surface every time the thought occurred to her.

Amanda brushed the tears from her suitcase and zipped it up. Lifting it from the bed, she slung her purse over her shoulder and left the room.

After placing the suitcase in the trunk of the car with the rest of her few possessions, she looked back at the big stone house for a brief moment. It had been home to her for almost two years. In truth, it had felt more like a real home than the one she had shared with her father.

Feeling the tears slide down her cheeks, she quickly settled into the driver's seat, turned the key in the ignition, and backed out of the driveway. If she hesitated much longer, she might succumb to the temptation to abandon her plans.

* * *

Drew was puzzled when he entered the house a few hours after Amanda's departure. She should have been home by now, but her car was not in the driveway nor in the garage. He walked directly to the telephone expecting to find a voice mail message explaining her delay, but when he lifted the receiver, he was greeted by the usual dial tone.

A few minutes later, he entered the bedroom and saw a note taped to the mirror. He had to read it twice before he fully understood its meaning.

Dear Drew,

I've decided I can't continue with our marriage. Please try to understand. I appreciate everything you've done for me, but it's time I learned to take care of myself. I know taking the money from the bank account is contradictory to that statement, but I'll repay you as soon as I can. You should be able to get a divorce without any trouble. I hope you'll be happy— you deserve it. Thank you again.

—Amanda

Drew shook his head in disbelief. What had prompted her to pick up and leave so abruptly? He had thought they were getting along so well lately. He admitted their relationship had been less than ideal at first. For months after they were married, he had some misgivings about making love to her because there was such a gap between their ages. In five years, that gap would not seem so wide, but her innocence and naivete made all the difference.

It was amazing that Amanda had not become hardened after dealing with her contemptible father. In spite of all she had been through and the harsh realities she had faced, she had seemed younger to Drew than her seventeen years. At twenty-four, his knowledge and worldliness far outdistanced hers, and that added to his guilt. He could not help but feel he was taking advantage of her. Although he had not admitted to an emotion as strong as love, his feelings for her had grown. He also knew their marriage would not survive if their relationship remained platonic. Even though she had not seemed hesitant about their physical relationship once she had overcome her initial nervousness, there had still been something missing. She accepted the intimacy, but he had the impression it was not very enjoyable for her.

Aside from his concerns about her reasons for leaving, he was worried about where she would go. He knew, without a doubt, that she would not return to her father's house; there was no reason for her to feel desperate enough to make that move. The only other possibility he could imagine was her friend, Nicole. Before he could act on his thought, the telephone rang.

"Hi, Drew," Nicole said. "May I speak to Amanda?"

Her question took him by surprise. So much for his hope to learn his wife's whereabouts so easily.

"She's not here, Nicole."

"Oh, I thought she would be home by now. Would you ask her to call me when she comes in?"

Drew hesitated. He had no desire to tell her that his wife had found their life together so distasteful, she'd left him. But he could see that he didn't have much choice. Nicole was sure to call back if Amanda did not return her call.

"She won't be coming back. She left. I was hoping she was with you."

"I haven't seen her since lunch. What do you mean, she left? What happened? Did you have an argument? What makes you think she won't be coming back?"

Drew appreciated the close friendship between Nicole and Amanda, but he felt the beginnings of resentment at her prying.

"She left a note," he said shortly.

Having blurted out the first response that came to her mind, Drew's tone of voice told her she had been insensitive.

"I'm sorry, Drew. I don't mean to pry. I'm just worried about her. I don't understand why she'd do this."

"Neither do I," he admitted with a sigh. "I'm concerned about her, too, Nicole. To answer your question, we didn't have an argument. I had no indication this was coming. How did she seem at lunch?"

"She seemed fine. She didn't confide anything to make me suspect she planned to leave."

They were both silent for a few seconds. "I'm sure she'll be okay, Drew," Nicole tried to assure him. "Amanda was pretty much taking care of herself for years before you came into her life."

"I know, but that doesn't keep me from worrying about her. I'm going to ask a favor of you, Nicole. You're her best friend, maybe her only friend aside from me. I'm sure she'll get in touch with you eventually. I'd appreciate it if you'd let me know when she does. I need to know that she's alright."

"I understand, Drew. I'll keep in touch and let you know how she's doing."

"Thanks, Nicole."

She sensed there was more involved than he confided. "I'm sorry, Drew. I hope you're right about her getting in touch with me."

For a long time after hanging up the telephone, Drew sat staring at the note. He was not prepared for the unexpected sense of loss. When had he fallen in love with Amanda?

When he'd married her, he had told himself it was

to rescue her from a tyrannical father. She never spoke of her mother, except to tell him that she had died when Amanda was only seven years old.

From what he had seen for himself, Amanda had never been completely cowed by her father. He learned something of her background from his father's secretary when Amanda had worked in his office. It must have been her mother who had instilled in her the courage and confidence she had always demonstrated. The lessons she had obviously taught her daughter had survived, in spite of the verbal abuse from her father. Drew had admired those traits from the first time he met her.

Drew glanced at the letter again, unable to bring himself to believe Amanda was gone from his life forever. Maybe when she was settled in her new life, she would contact him. Even if she was too upset or embarrassed to contact him, he was sure she would contact Nicole.

Once he learned her whereabouts, he could go after her and try to convince her to return. But would that really be fair to either of them? And what would he do, how would he feel, if she refused?

Feelings of anger rose to the surface. She could have told him she was unhappy with their relationship. They could have discussed the problems, whatever they were. She had to have been very unhappy to take such a drastic step.

With that thought he stifled the anger, trying to see the situation from her point of view. Although his conscience was clear in the knowledge that he had treated her well, he could not say the same for his family. His mother had made no secret of her resentment toward Amanda and displeasure with the marriage. She had taken every opportunity to belittle

her, and maybe Amanda was not convinced that he
did not share his mother's opinions.

There was also the fact that she had been forced
into the marriage. He could imagine she felt trapped
and could see no other way of escape.

Drew read the note again. She said she needed to
learn to take care of herself. Nicole's statement had
reinforced his own opinion that she had been doing
that for most of her young life. Evidently, she did not
see it that way.

Whatever her real reasons for leaving, his main
concern at the moment was her well-being. He could
do nothing about that until she contacted him or
Nicole. Once he knew she was well, he could hope
for more. He could not keep from hoping that one
day she would come back into his life.

One

Amanda gathered the files from the table and prepared to leave the conference room. She was pleased with the reports she had given. There was still work to be done, but significant progress had been made. At least she had planted some important seeds over the past months. Seeds that would give her charges a better chance of growing into well-adjusted, confident adults.

The director of the center caught up with her as she reached the door. "I'm really glad to see the progress in Danita, Amanda. I've talked to her myself so I know, firsthand, what a difference you've made."

"I have to confess, Sharon. Danita was one of the easier ones to reach. The children whose parents bring them here voluntarily, out of concern, are always the easiest to turn around."

"That may be true, but I think you underestimate your ability. You seem to have a real talent for recognizing exactly what a child needs."

"Actually, you and I both know that what most of these kids need is basically the same thing, self-esteem. Finding a way to instill it in them is the real problem."

Sharon nodded. "It makes all the difference when the parents are willing to work with us, and learn

good parenting skills. There are too many situations
where that isn't the case, not just with our patients."

When Amanda arrived home that evening, there
was a phone message from Nicole. She and Nicole
had been friends since second grade. Nicole had always been there for her, and she had kept in touch
even when she moved to Chester from Philadelphia.
She had needed to get away from her marriage, but
she could not bring herself to put hundreds of miles
between herself and everyone she knew.

When Amanda left Drew, she originally planned to
break all ties with her previous life. She changed her
mind almost immediately upon settling into her new
home. Aside from the loneliness, she had realized
she could not do that to her friend. She imagined
how worried Nicole would be, not knowing where
she was or if she was alright. She could not be that
unfair to her friend, or to herself.

Amanda remembered how unnecessarily she had
worried about that first call to Nicole. She would not
have blamed her friend if she had refused to speak
to her. Nicole's only reaction was relief to hear from
her. There was no indication of reproach.

After their initial conversation, they called each
other frequently. Amanda never mentioned Drew,
and Nicole refrained from asking any disturbing
questions.

There were times, even now, when Amanda felt
guilty for the way she had treated Drew. She admitted
to herself she had not been entirely fair to him. Her
decision to sneak off during his absence, leaving only
a note to explain her departure, had given her more
than a few moments of uneasiness.

Hindsight had made her more objective about her

actions. She could, and probably should, have been more open with him. Her mind was in such a state of turmoil when she left that an open discussion had not been an option. She simply could not face him then and explain her reason for leaving. If she had had the courage to do that, she might have had the courage to stay.

After she was settled, she dialed her friend's number. "What's up girlfriend? I got your message.."

"I'm getting married."

"Congratulations! I assume the lucky man is the perfect David."

"Of course, who else? He proposed last night. I called to invite you to the engagement party and to ask you to be my maid of honor."

"You know I'll be there. I'll be happy to be your maid of honor under one condition. You have to promise not to pick some hideous antebellum-style gown for the bridesmaids."

"I promise. In fact, I'll even let you choose the gown."

The two women chatted for more than an hour before they finally hung up. Amanda smiled at her friend's excitement. She was truly happy for her, but felt a little wistful.

If she had not run away, could she have experienced that same happiness? Did she throw away the chance that Drew might, eventually, fall in love with her?

That thought had plagued her off and on for six years, and each time, she pushed the idea aside. She remembered how long it had taken him to consummate the marriage. When he finally did, it had seemed that his heart was not really in it. She was mature enough now to admit there was a possibility that her own reaction to his advances might have had something to do with his hesitancy. She had held

back, afraid he would guess how much she loved him.
For him, it was only a matter of physical need and
the convenience of having a wife to fulfill that need.

She sighed. "What's that old saying about spilled
milk?" she murmured to herself.

Her mind wandered back to the beginning, the
first time she met Drew. She was just sixteen, working
part-time as a clerk in his father's company. She developed an immediate crush on the young man. His
unfailing kindness and apparent concern for her future had served to increase her infatuation.

Even at sixteen, she was realistic enough to recognize it as a crush. She was content simply to be near
him. She never, in her wildest dreams, considered
the possibility of marriage to him. She had her father
to thank for that eventuality.

Her father, who had never paid much attention to
her except to accuse her of some wrongdoing. Her
father, who had always been eager to assume the
worst. His threats had coerced Drew into proposing
marriage.

She never had any illusions that Drew was in love
with her. He told her he was "fond" of her. He suggested that marriage to him was her means of escape
from a home situation that was likely to become even
more intolerable.

Amanda had expected they would get a divorce
when he found out the truth about the baby, or an
annulment, since he appeared to have no desire to
consummate the marriage. She was surprised when
he suggested, instead, that they could make the marriage work.

For a while, she thought he might be right. Before
long, her teenage infatuation matured into love. That
realization and the knowledge that he did not return
her love made it unbearable to continue to live with

him. It was only a matter of time before her true feelings would be exposed. On one hand, she could stay with him and hope that his "fondness" would grow into love, but that seemed unlikely.

She could not continue to live with him for years, day after day, knowing her feelings were one-sided. She knew the longer she stayed, the harder it would be to live with the situation, and even more difficult to leave him.

The weekend after her telephone conversation with Amanda, Nicole and her mother went shopping for her gown. A few minutes after they had pulled out of her mother's driveway, Nicole mentioned her call to Amanda.

"She agreed to be my maid of honor, not that I really expected her to refuse. She'll be here for the engagement party, too."

Charlotte nodded. "That's great, honey."

Nicole glanced sidelong at the older woman. "You don't sound very enthusiastic."

"It's not that. I just wondered if you happened to mention to her the name of your best man."

"He's not *my* best man, Mom. I had no control over the choice."

"That wasn't my question, Nicole."

Nicole sighed. She was not deceived by the soft tone of her mother's voice. Her mother was not pleased with the omission.

"No, Mom, I didn't tell her the name of the best man."

Two months after Nicole's telephone call, Amanda arrived in Philadelphia for the engagement party. Although Nicole had visited her several times, Amanda had not returned to her hometown since she moved away six years earlier except for a few visits to the art museums. After checking the directions Nicole had given her, she drove directly to her friend's apartment.

Nicole greeted her with a hug. "It's so good to see you again. It's been too long. Telephone calls just aren't enough. I hope you're prepared to be awake half the night."

"I'm prepared. I didn't expect it to be any different than the times you've visited me. As long as you promise not to wake me before noon tomorrow. After all, I have to get my beauty rest for the party tomorrow night."

"What about me? It's my party."

"True, but I'm sure David won't care if you have a few dark circles under your eyes."

As they expected, it was the wee hours of the morning before the two friends finally went to bed. Nicole had refrained from any further comment when Amanda informed her she had no intention of visiting her father. As far as Amanda was concerned, she and her father had nothing to discuss.

Amanda had not voiced her concern about the possibility of encountering Drew. It was a big city. She had no intention of going anywhere near his office or the neighborhood where they had lived. She was convinced the likelihood of coming into contact with her former husband was remote.

The afternoon after Amanda's arrival was spent shopping for the bridesmaids' gowns. Although her friend had promised Amanda that she could choose the style, the decision was not hers alone. Two of the bridesmaids met them at the store.

Nicole showed them the gown she had chosen for herself, a full-skirted vision with a beaded lace bodice and long train. After some discussion, they agreed on a sheath style in sapphire-blue satin. The basic style of all the gowns was the same. The only difference was that the bodice of Amanda's gown had a square neckline, while the others had a mock wrap bodice with a vee neckline. The women all agreed that a slight variation for the maid of honor would not ruin the uniformity of the total picture.

That evening, Amanda learned that even a city as large as Philadelphia was not big enough to protect her from the meeting she had hoped to avoid. A few minutes after her arrival at the party, she was caught off guard by a familiar voice behind her.

"Hello, Amanda."

She spun around and found herself face-to-face with Drew. She fought the urge to take a deep breath when she looked into eyes so black the irises were indistinguishable from the pupils. Those same eyes had haunted her dreams for six years.

"What are you doing here?"

Drew smiled, revealing the dimple that had always fascinated her. "It's good to see you, too."

He was standing less than a foot away from her. Looking into the eyes Amanda knew so well was difficult in itself, but the added smile was devastating. She tried to regain her composure as the heat crept up her neck.

Her memory had not served her well. He was even more handsome than she remembered. He seemed taller than the six-foot-two inches in her mind's image from six years ago. The skin was the same, though, like creamy-smooth milk chocolate. No man had the right to have such beautiful skin.

In their long conversation the previous night, Nicole never mentioned that he had been invited to the party. She wondered if her friend had deliberately planned this meeting.

Drew understood her embarrassment at being taken by surprise. He could only imagine his own reaction if the tables were turned. He was grateful that he had seen her across the room before she spied him, even though he already had the upper hand. Knowing how close she was to Nicole, he knew it was unlikely she would miss her friend's wedding.

For six years he had been telling himself she would come back into his life. He had been tempted a few times in the past year to take matters into his own hands and simply show up on her doorstep, unannounced. When David had told him he and Nicole were engaged, Drew knew the event would bring them face-to-face again.

He murmured her name and Amanda realized she had been staring speechlessly for too long. "I didn't mean that the way it sounded. I was just surprised to see you. I didn't know you were a friend of the Jessups."

"I'm not really. David and I are good friends. We were roommates in college. I'm his best man."

"Oh," she murmured, finally tearing her eyes away. She could think of nothing else to say to him at that moment, although she promised herself she would have a few choice words for her friend. If he was the best man, then Nicole knew he would be at the party.

Drew could not take his eyes off of her. He had watched her from across the room earlier in the evening, waiting patiently as she mingled with the other guests. He knew that eventually, he would find an opportunity to speak with her alone.

Her hair was shorter than he recalled. Parted slightly to the side and brushed back from her face, it fell in soft waves that skimmed her shoulders. He wanted to reach out and touch the smooth, caramel-hued skin revealed by the low-cut neckline. Even more tempting was the glimpse of cleavage. That was another characteristic he did not remember from years earlier.

"How long will you be in town? Maybe we could have dinner."

"I'm leaving tomorrow afternoon."

"How about lunch then?"

"I don't think so. I have a few things to take care of before I leave." Before she was tempted to reconsider his invitation, she excused herself and made her escape.

Drew stared appreciatively as she retreated. The well-rounded figure in the silk emerald-green sheath was a delightful change from that of the teenager he had met years ago. Aside from the physical changes, and in spite of her uneasiness, he sensed the confidence and self-assurance that had increased in the years since her flight.

His appearance had startled her, but they were even. The desire that welled up in him at the sight of her had taken him by surprise. When she refused his invitation, he felt the first stirrings of anger. He suspected she was simply looking for an excuse to avoid him, but she could not avoid him forever. She would be back for the wedding. He had waited more than six years; he could wait a few more months. He was determined to get to the bottom of her real reason for leaving him. Although she might not agree, he felt she owed him that much.

The night was full of surprises for Amanda. She had not expected Drew to be at the party. She certainly would never have imagined he would invite her to dinner. At first, she half expected he would be angry at her sudden departure years earlier. Then it occurred to her that she was being unrealistic. There was no reason for him to be angry. It was not as if he had any deep feelings for her, and she had repaid the money years ago. Besides, there had been more than enough time for any anger to dissipate.

On the other hand, if he was angry for some reason, she could not be certain that it had dissipated. Their brief conversation was not enough to make that determination. Since he was not the type of person to make a scene in a public place, his calm demeanor was no indication of his true emotions.

As for the dinner invitation, she supposed it was only natural that he would be curious about her. She had certainly had her share of thoughts about him. Which was exactly why she worked very hard to avoid being alone with him the rest of the evening.

After her encounter with Drew, Amanda looked around for his parents and sister. She was sure his family would have been invited, but it would not have surprised her if his parents had decided that this gathering was not worth their precious time.

"Why didn't you tell me about Drew?" Amanda asked her friend later that night as they prepared for bed.

Nicole shrugged. "I'm not really sure. I guessed that you wouldn't be happy about it. Maybe I was just a little afraid you'd refuse to be in my wedding."

Amanda stared at her. "You're not serious? How could you think that? We've been friends since we were kids. You've been there for me through everything."

"Alright, alright. I didn't really think you'd let me down."

"It's not easy to admit, Nicole, but I think you're the only real friend I've ever had. That's why you were the only one I contacted when I left here. I knew I couldn't just disappear and not tell you where I was."

"I worried about that for a while. Even though you didn't explain why you left, I never expected that you wouldn't have had any contact with him at all. After a while I had the impression you were avoiding him, since you never even mentioned his name. I didn't know how to tell you I'd be the one responsible for bringing you face-to-face with him after all these years. Was it really that bad seeing him again?"

Amanda shrugged. "No, I was just surprised," she lied.

"Am I forgiven?"

"Of course, you're forgiven. It's not that important. By the way, why weren't his parents or sister at the party? I thought they'd have been invited since he's in the wedding."

"They were invited. His sister called Thursday to tell me she had the flu, and his parents are vacationing in Hawaii. It might sound terrible, but I can't say I'm sorry they couldn't be here."

"I'm sure I don't have to tell you that I second that opinion."

Two

The effects of her encounter with Drew lingered with Amanda for months after her return home. Memories of him intruded at the most inopportune moments during the day, as if it were not enough that her dreams at night were filled with his image.

"Amanda? Are you still with us?"

Amanda forced her attention back to the discussion taking place in the center's conference room. Her preoccupation was merely another example of the extent to which her concentration had been taxed since returning from Philadelphia. She was saved from an embarrassing situation when one of her coworkers spoke up.

"Does Lisa know how long she'll be out?"

"She can't be sure. From what the doctor said, she's anticipating at least three months. I'm aware that some of you have other contracts to fulfill elsewhere. I need to know if the three of you will be able to handle any of her appointments and, if so, how many you think you can take."

"I can probably take a few of her appointments if we can rearrange the schedule," Amanda volunteered. "The school year is winding down, so I won't be needed there much longer. If Lisa's not back by September there might be a problem, though."

At the moment, Amanda welcomed the additional work. It would help keep her mind occupied during the summer months when she would no longer have her counseling duties with the school district.

The discussion continued for another hour and in the end, they managed to devise a schedule that was acceptable. It would mean limiting new patients, but if necessary they could be referred to another psychologist.

Amanda's plan for her busy summer schedule to keep her mind off Drew was not entirely successful. Although her work held her full attention during the day, nothing could erase him from her mind. She had managed to push him to the back of her mind when she left six years earlier, but seeing him again had re-kindled all the memories of their first meeting and the events that had led to their marriage.

She had never forgotten that day in his office when he proposed marriage. He had been coerced into it when her father stormed into his office, accusing him of being the father of her unborn child. Her father ended his tirade by threatening to take legal action against Drew because of her age.

For weeks before that confrontation, she had tried to convince her father that there was no child, that she was not pregnant. She had no idea what was responsible for her recurring nausea, but she knew she was not pregnant. She had no luck convincing her father of this and she finally stopped denying it. Eventually, it would become evident that he was mistaken. She could only hope that it would put an end to his hints that there was something between her and Drew.

At first, she did not understand why he had picked Drew as a likely candidate. His reasoning became clear when he mentioned seeing Drew drop her off at home one evening. But it had been raining hard and the young man had insisted there was no reason for her to get drenched, waiting for the bus. That one instance and the fact that she worked in his father's office had sent her father's imagination into gear.

When her father started his tirade against Drew, she tried, once more, to convince him. As usual, he turned a deaf ear to her denials. She then tried to explain to Drew that her father was mistaken. She was surprised, and hurt, when it appeared that he did not believe her, either.

It soon became clear that what her father really wanted was money, stressing the fact that "babies are expensive." He was looking for more than a weekly child support check from Drew for the baby, insisting that the initial needs preparing for the baby would be costly. That also explained one of his reasons for choosing Drew as a scapegoat. And Drew's offer of marriage shocked them both.

Drew then insisted upon speaking with her privately, and he explained his reasons for proposing marriage. At first, he was only interested in helping her by trying to make her life a little easier. Later, he truly tried to make the marriage work. How could she blame him for not falling in love with her? Love was uncontrollable, and her own feelings were a very good example.

Before leaving home for the wedding, Amanda tried to prepare herself for another encounter with Drew. She reminded herself that, in his own words years earlier, he wanted to be her friend. That and curiosity were probably the only motives behind his overtures. Whatever his motives, she had to remember that he did not share her feelings. She was still in love with him. There was nothing she could do except live with it, as she had done for the past six years. Unrequited love might be painful, but it was not fatal.

The evening of the wedding rehearsal, Amanda finished dressing and sat on the side of the bed watching her friend across the room. "I can't believe you're so calm. Aren't brides supposed to be a bundle of nerves?"

Nicole finished applying her lipstick and smiled. "Don't jinx me. This is just the rehearsal. I'm not sure I'll be this calm tomorrow."

She paused a moment. "Even if some minor problem comes up, though, I don't think I'll freak out. The only important things are that David and the minister show up at the church tomorrow and nothing happens to my family or friends. Nothing else really matters."

She turned from the mirror and looked at Amanda. "Speaking of bundles of nerves, how are you?"

Amanda focused her attention on the items she was putting in her purse. "I'm fine. I have no reason to be nervous."

"Tell that to someone else, girlfriend. I remember your reaction the last time you came face-to-face with Drew."

"I told you that was only because I was surprised to see him."

"Uh-huh. If you say so."

Drew was the first person Amanda saw when she entered the church. He was standing in the foyer talking to one of the other groomsmen. If she had hoped for a few more minutes to collect her thoughts, it was not to be. He broke off the conversation and came toward her.

He took her hand in his while he greeted Nicole and David, as if he expected her to bolt. For a few seconds after spotting him, she had considered and rejected that childish option. She just had to keep her emotions in check for the next few days.

"I'm glad to see you. I hope we'll have time for that dinner while you're here. I understand you'll be here for a few days."

She looked at Nicole. Her friend smiled and urged David into the sanctuary. Amanda was sure she had Nicole to thank for revealing her plans to remain in town for a few days.

"Yes, I'm leaving Tuesday. Mrs. Jessup thought it might be a big help to catalog the gifts before Nicole and David return from the honeymoon, and I offered to help."

"Catalog the gifts?"

Amanda shrugged. "I guess that's what you'd call it. You know, listing each gift and who sent it. It makes it a little easier for them to send the thank-you notes."

"Well, that shouldn't take all day, whichever day you choose to do it. Will you have dinner with me on Sunday?"

There was no point in continuing to refuse him. "Sure, dinner Sunday sounds fine."

"Is this cataloging part of your duties as maid of honor?"

"Not really, just a favor."

"I've been wondering, shouldn't you be called the matron of honor? Although, I have to admit the term 'matron' doesn't fit you."

"Actually, I'm not sure. I know a married woman

is matron of honor; I'm not sure of the proper title for a divorced woman."

Drew cleared his throat and looked down at his feet. He knew he should have told her the truth a long time ago. He opened his mouth to explain, but they were interrupted by the wedding coordinator. It was time for the rehearsal to start.

When it came time for Amanda to join Drew in her march down the aisle, she steeled herself for the physical contact. She recalled the tingling she felt earlier when he had held her hand.

Drew was aware of the slight trembling of her hand when she took his arm. He mistook it for a minor case of nerves and placed his own hand over hers to reassure her. He was puzzled when that action seemed to increase the trembling rather than ease it.

Amanda relaxed a little at the rehearsal dinner. Being in the company of other people rather than alone with him helped ease the tension. That realization gave her second thoughts about accepting his invitation to dinner.

The only problem at the moment was that they were seated directly across from each other and it was difficult to keep her eyes off of him. At least that was the only problem until he urged her onto the dance floor after dinner, effectively destroying any possibility of controlling her wayward emotions.

He took her in his arms and her heart began beating in double time. Amanda made the mistake of closing her eyes, and the scent and feel of him recalled the sensual memories of their short time together. It took all her powers of concentration to maintain her composure.

After dinner, Drew insisted on driving her back to Nicole's apartment. Her friend had left earlier because, as she said, she needed her beauty rest or her "something blue" would be the circles under her eyes.

When they reached the door of the apartment, Amanda rummaged in her purse for the key Nicole had given her. Drew promptly took it from her hand and unlocked the door. Amanda reached for the knob and his hand closed over hers. She looked up questioningly and saw in his eyes what she had over-looked until that moment—desire. Seconds later, he lowered his head and captured her lips in a sweet, but searing, kiss. She was still in a trance when he opened the door and gently urged her inside.

"Good night, Amanda."

Drew walked down the hallway smiling. The kiss had answered a question that had been in his mind all day. The look in her eyes and her reaction indi-cated she felt the same desire that had plagued him since the previous evening. In truth, it had plagued him even in her absence.

In the past six years, he had gone months at a time without consciously thinking about her. Inevitably, when he least expected it, she would appear in his dreams. Having held her in his arms again, he ad-mitted that his dreams had been severely lacking.

His smile faded when he recalled their conversation in the church, and he felt guilty at not telling her the truth. He tried to excuse his omission by telling himself that there had been no time before the rehearsal. Deep down, he knew it was not a valid excuse. He could have made time later at the rehearsal dinner.

The next morning sped by with the wedding prepa-rations. Amanda tried to keep her mind on the busi-ness at hand, namely getting dressed and made-up. After ending the previous evening with the discovery that Drew's motivations included more than curiosity or friendship, it was not surprising that her dreams had been filled with images of him. Those mental images had carried over into her waking moments and the entire morning.

"Can you help me with these buttons please, Amanda?"

"Sure."

"I don't know what I was thinking of when I bought this gown. Of course, I knew I didn't have to worry about trying to button it myself. I knew my good friend would be here to help."

"Right. David might not appreciate having to unbutton them all tonight, though."

"Oh, I don't know. He might actually appreciate it. You know what they say about anticipation."

Amanda laughed. "Are you basing your opinion on what you've heard or is this from your own experience? And if you're basing it on your own experience, are you sure it works both ways?"

"Well if not, I'll be sewing about thirty buttons back on this dress."

There was no sign of Drew when they entered the church, but Amanda spotted his parents entering the sanctuary. She no longer felt the hurt and anger she had suffered when she and Drew were together. It had taken a few years for her to realize that his mother was the real problem, and that she was not to blame for the older woman's dislike of her. She had long ago reached the conclusion that Mrs. Connors would dislike any woman Drew married. No one would be good enough.

Drew's mother had also seen her former daughter-in-law, but she refrained from any comment until they were seated.

"Did you know about this, Kenneth?" she whispered through clenched teeth.

Her husband sighed inwardly and feigned ignorance. "Know about what, dear?"

"That girl. Evidently, she's in the wedding."

"If you mean Amanda, no, I wasn't aware she was in the wedding. I'm not surprised, though. I understand she and Nicole are the best of friends."

"How do you know so much? And why didn't you tell me?"

"I know because I ask questions, Claire, and I listen to our son."

Claire glanced sharply at him, but he stared straight ahead. His words had sounded almost like a reproach. She dismissed the possibility. Kenneth would never reprove her. She had to have misunderstood his meaning.

The wedding ceremony proceeded with no problems. In the beginning, Amanda could not take her eyes off of Drew, breathtaking in his tuxedo. In all the years she had known him, she had never seen him in evening clothes.

She remembered her own wedding. It had been nothing like the grand affair she was witnessing now. At her request, she and Drew had been married in a church, but the only ones in attendance had been Nicole, Mr. and Mrs. Jessup, and Drew's sister, Jennifer. Amanda had been surprised that Jennifer had asked to be included. She later understood that the young woman did not share her parents' opinion of Drew's decision.

Her attention was drawn away from Drew when Nicole and David repeated their vows. Amanda tried, unobtrusively, to wipe away a stray tear. Whether it was from happiness for her friend or disappointment over the break-up of her own marriage, she was not sure. She became aware that her attempt to hide her emotions had been unsuccessful when she looked up and saw Drew watching her.

For the remainder of the evening, she was naturally paired with Drew by virtue of their positions in the wedding party. But she made up her mind to enjoy the evening and not let the past intrude.

When Drew drove Amanda back to Nicole's apartment, she recalled the previous night's kiss. The fact that she was hoping for a repeat of that incident told her she was playing with fire.

After seeing Amanda safely into the apartment, Drew turned to leave. He heard a faint sigh and turned back to face her. He guessed that she was totally unaware of the desire revealed in her eyes.

When he took her in his arms, all of Amanda's reservations disappeared. She had almost convinced herself that the previous evening's kiss had only been so powerful because it was unexpected. However, the jolt of awareness that vibrated through her body when his lips touched hers totally banished that conviction.

Drew's arms tightened around her, pulling her closer. She entwined her arms around his neck as his tongue outlined her full trembling lips before seeking access to the sweet nectar he had tasted much too briefly the previous night.

She sighed when he broke the kiss. She wanted more. Her arms were still entwined around his neck and she unconsciously tightened them, pulling his head down until his lips were less than an inch from her own.

Drew would have enjoyed nothing more than to

carry this encounter to its logical conclusion, but he knew it was too soon. There were too many questions still unanswered, and one important piece of information he had neglected to give her.

He planted a brief, chaste kiss on her lips. Any more than that would seriously jeopardize his resolve to proceed slowly. He smiled at the look of disappointment on her face.

"I think I'd better leave while I still have some control. Don't forget we have a dinner date tomorrow. I'll pick you up at seven."

A moment later he was gone, and Amanda was left with more questions than ever. His comment about losing control had not escaped her. It had reinforced her opinion that she had not mistaken the desire in his eyes.

Three

The next day, Amanda drove to the Jessups' house. Many gifts already had been delivered, and the Jessups had taken the gifts from the reception home the previous night.

It had been years since Amanda had visited the Jessups' home. They had moved from Amanda's neighborhood three years before her marriage to Drew. Although she and Nicole kept in touch by phone, she had only visited a few times afterward. Before leaving the apartment, she called Mrs. Jessup for directions.

Charlotte greeted her with a hug. "I'm glad you volunteered to help me with this. Not just for the obvious reasons. Things have been so hectic for the past few days, I haven't had a chance to talk to you."

"I can imagine. But everything was really beautiful."

"Thanks. More important than that, I think everyone had a good time."

After taking Amanda's coat, Charlotte directed her to the dining room. "I cleared the dining room table for us. Can I get you anything before we start? Have you eaten?"

"I ate just before leaving the apartment."

"How about coffee? I just made a fresh pot."

"That sounds fine."

The two women worked for a while before Charlotte began gently probing. "I hope you weren't too upset about Drew being in the wedding. I told Nicole she should warn you ahead of time. She knew he was a friend of David's, but it wasn't until they started making plans that she learned they were close enough for David to ask him to be best man."

"I wasn't upset, just a little surprised."

"I must say, the two of you seemed to get along. I expected to see some signs of antagonism."

She hesitated, but Amanda made no comment. "Or maybe you just kept those feelings to yourself for Nicole's sake."

"No, Mrs. Jessup. I was never angry with Drew. My reasons for leaving had nothing to do with his treatment of me."

Charlotte sensed that that was as far as her daughter's friend would go. It was enough. It answered the most important question that had been in her mind for years. She did not want to think she had misjudged the young man who had appeared to be so kind and caring.

By five-thirty that evening, Amanda was back in her friend's apartment, trying to decide on an outfit for dinner. The possibility of a dinner date had never entered her mind when she was packing for this trip, and her options were limited. She decided on the navy shawl-collared, double-breasted coatdress she had packed as a possible alternative for the wedding rehearsal. Her silver necklace with a lapis lazuli pendant, matching earrings, navy pumps and clutch bag completed the outfit.

She was applying her lipstick when she heard a knock at the door. She went to the door, then took a deep breath before opening it to Drew. He was wearing gray slacks and a navy jacket. His white shirt was open at the neck, revealing a glimpse of smooth brown skin.

He leaned over and kissed her cheek as he entered. "You look beautiful," he murmured.

"Thank you. I wasn't sure what to wear. Not that I had a lot to choose from."

His gaze traveled the length of her body. "You managed extremely well."

Amanda's pulse rate increased under his scrutiny. Earlier, she had considered the possibility of taking a sweater, in case the air-conditioning in the restaurant became uncomfortable. If he continued to look at her in that way, she might be the one requesting to have the air-conditioning turned up.

Drew knew it was time for the revelation he had been withholding. He waited until they had finished their meal.

"I'm glad you accepted my invitation. We haven't really had much opportunity to talk privately. There's an important matter we need to discuss." He looked down at his plate for a moment and then raised his head, looking her straight in the eye. "Amanda, do you remember when you mentioned that you weren't sure if a divorced woman would be considered a maid of honor or a matron of honor?"

Amanda looked puzzled. "Yes. Why?"

"Because I have a confession to make. I should have told you before now. In spite of the fact that we've had little chance for private conversation, I guess I don't really have a good excuse for not telling you."

He took a deep breath. "What I'm trying to say is, it doesn't matter what the proper term is for a divorced woman."

"What do you mean?"

"You're still married."

Amanda stared at him. "What, exactly, does that mean?"

He took a deep breath. "I think you know what it means. I never got a divorce."

"You're joking! You must be joking."

"I'm not joking, Amanda. I wouldn't joke about that. Think about it. Did you get any papers to sign?"

She shook her head. "It seems so easy to get a divorce these days, I thought the letter I signed would be all you'd need. I never expected to receive any papers, since you didn't know where to contact me. I'm sorry if you had a problem getting a divorce."

"That's not why I didn't get the divorce, Amanda. I've always known where you were. I made it my business to know."

"Why?"

Drew sighed. He had known this wouldn't be simple. "I was concerned about you. You were eighteen years old and you had been through a lot. You had no relatives other than your father and I knew you wouldn't go back to his house. I was thankful that, at least, you had some money."

"You were thankful that I took your money?"

"It wasn't my money, Amanda. I gave it to you."

"You put it in the account to pay for college."

"Did you go to college?"

"Well, yes, but that's not the point."

Drew smiled. "That is the point. It wasn't necessary for you to repay the money."

Amanda looked down at her empty plate. "I expected you to be angry."

"I guess I was a little angry at first, but not about the money. I was more worried than angry."

"You mentioned that you've always known where

I lived. In that case, why didn't you tell me about your decision not to get a divorce? I might have committed bigamy, thinking I was divorced."

"I knew Nicole would tell me if you had become seriously involved with another man."

"I assume I have Nicole to thank for the fact that you knew so much about my life after I left."

"Yes, but I hope you won't hold it against her. I was worried about you, and she simply reassured me that you were okay."

Amanda shook her head. "No, I won't hold it against her. I guess I wasn't really surprised that she would tell you. I was just a little surprised that you bothered. When you mentioned the money I took, I had the impression you knew I went to college. I guess she told you that, too."

"Yes, but not much more than that. What did you study?"

"Child psychology. And I'm working in my field."

"Doing what?"

"I work at a center that counsels problem children. I also do some counseling for the school district."

Drew smiled. "I should have known you'd be involved with helping children. I think that's great, but it must be hard sometimes."

"Sometimes, but it's worth it."

Amanda hesitated a moment. Their conversation had veered off from its original topic, namely the fact that they were not divorced. She steered it back. She was not sure she wanted to hear the answer to the question in her mind, but she had to ask.

"Drew, the fact that you never filed for a divorce raises another question."

She looked away from him, fearful of seeing the truth in his eyes. "Why you didn't file for a divorce? Was it because you still felt sorry for me?"

"No, Amanda. I don't think I ever really felt sorry for you. I was concerned about you."

He reached across the table and took her hand in his. His other hand cupped her chin, forcing her to meet his gaze. "I guess the main reason I never filed for divorce was because I didn't want to break the tie between us. The truth is, I'm still not ready to break the tie. I'd like very much for us to get reacquainted."

His thumb absently caressed the back of her hand, and Amanda had difficulty forming a coherent thought.

"I'm going back home on Tuesday."

He smiled. "You have a telephone, don't you? And you don't live that far away. So, how about it?"

"Drew, I think you're ignoring an important element. You have to understand that I'm not the same person you knew six years ago."

"I should hope not. I hope that we've both grown, but I don't believe a person's basic personality changes. Besides, that's the whole idea of getting reacquainted. Will you give it—give us—a chance?"

Amanda wanted nothing more than to believe they really had a chance to make their relationship work. She refused to consider how she would feel if this attempt did not succeed. She loved him. It seemed she had loved him all her life. If there was the slightest possibility of making their marriage work, she had to try. She had thrown away that chance years earlier; she would not make that mistake again.

"Yes, Drew. I'd like for us to get reacquainted."

Drew wasted no time in following up on his suggestion that they renew their relationship. He called her twice in the week after she returned home. When he called on Thursday, he suggested they go out to dinner on Saturday.

She was dressed when he arrived, and they left a few minutes later. He had not asked for any restaurant suggestions from her, and when he drove to the I-95 North entrance, she was surprised.

"Where are we going?"

"I made reservations at the *Moshulu*. Have you ever been there?"

"Only once, about a year ago, for a teacher's retirement party."

The restaurant was actually a four-masted sailing ship that had been converted into a restaurant some years earlier. It was moored at a pier on the Delaware River near the recreation area of Penn's Landing in Philadelphia.

Dinner was a quiet, relaxing affair. There was no more discussion about the past. She learned that his father was now semi-retired. Drew had taken charge of the insurance brokerage firm the older man had established. In addition to the usual insurance, the company handled a variety of investment options.

When he talked about the company, it occurred to her that his family's financial status might be the basis of a great deal of his mother's resentment toward her. When they married eight years ago, she had been a teenager and a nobody as far his parents were concerned. They had probably seen her as a gold digger, or at the least a calculating manipulator looking to take advantage of their son's compassion.

Even if that had been the case, surely they must realize there was no chance of that now. It should be obvious that she was independent, that she was a success in her own right. Her financial success might not equal his, but she was a capable and respected child psychologist. Maybe now they would accept the fact that all she wanted was his love.

After dinner, they spent a half hour in the lounge dancing to the live music. They both seemed reluctant to end the evening. Before leaving, Drew suggested a stroll on the boardwalk. The sprinkling of lights on the bridge a short distance away glittered against the cloudless sky and cast their reflections on the water.

They stood at the railing watching the lights as the excursion ship, *The Spirit of Philadelphia,* passed by. Drew first became aware of the drop in temperature when he felt her shiver slightly in the shelter of his arm.

"I think we'd better be going. I don't want to be responsible for your catching cold."

When Drew returned her to her apartment, he stayed just long enough to see her safely inside. Amanda was disappointed, even more so after he said good-bye with a long, searing kiss.

The following week, it was the same. They had dinner at a small restaurant near her apartment, but he left immediately after seeing her home. Amanda was beginning to wonder if she had misread the desire she had seen in his eyes on more than one occasion. Aside from the kisses that made her weak in the knees, he had made no other advances.

On his third visit, she insisted upon cooking dinner for them. He arrived early that afternoon, offering to help, but she insisted she had the preparations under control.

"The roast is ready to go in the oven, and the salad is in refrigerator. You won't have to feel guilty about relaxing and watching the football game."

Drew laughed. "Well, if you insist. Are you going to join me?"

"Sure. It's not my favorite pastime, but I don't mind watching."

The game had just ended when she informed him that dinner was ready. "That's what I call perfect timing. Did you plan it this way?"

"Actually, it's been ready for about fifteen minutes. I noticed the game was getting down to the wire and I didn't have the heart to interrupt you."

When they returned to the living room after dinner, the television was still on, but neither of them seemed very interested in it. Amanda flipped half-heartedly through the channels for a few minutes until Drew pulled her into his arms and onto his lap.

Even if she had wanted to, there was no time to protest. Drew's mouth came down on hers, making speech impossible. Her arms entwined his neck as he pulled her closer.

His hand stroked her back before finding its way under her sweater to cup her breast, gently teasing the sensitive nub through the fabric of her bra. She moaned softly when it hardened beneath his touch. It was all the encouragement he needed.

His hand moved to her thigh and eased beneath the fabric of her skirt, stroking up and down. His fingers worked their way around the soft flesh and came to rest at the warm juncture of her thighs.

Amanda gasped. She was not ready for this. She placed her hand on his, pulling it from its resting place. Unable to look him in the eye, she hid her face in his shoulder.

"I can't do this, Drew. I'm sorry. I thought I was ready for this, but I'm not."

Although the thumping of her heart next to his seemed to contradict her statement, the embarrassment in her voice told him she was right to put an end to their lovemaking. As long as she had any reservations, the time was not right.

After adjusting her skirt, he held her for a moment. Then, easing her head from his shoulder, he leaned back and looked at her face. Her eyes were still closed, but her cheeks were streaked with tears.

"Amanda, it's alright. I've wanted to make love to you for months. I guess I got carried away."

She shook her head. "It's not your fault. I wanted it, too, and I thought I was ready. I guess I'm not. I shouldn't have let it get this far."

"In that case, I guess we both got carried away."

She struggled to get up from his lap. He helped her onto the sofa beside him. Taking her hand in one of his, he lifted her chin.

"Amanda I won't allow you to feel guilty about this. It's not the end of the world, nor the end of this relationship."

"Do you have any idea how embarrassing this is?"

Drew was painfully aware of his own physical condition. "I think I just might."

The look on his face was more telling than his words. She closed her eyes. "Oh, Drew."

He laughed and hugged her. "Amanda, honey, I'll survive. Believe me, I'll survive because I intend to be right here when you are ready."

Drew thought he had finally convinced her that he was not upset. "I think it's time for me to leave, though. Otherwise, we'll be back where we were a few minutes ago."

Still looking uncertain, she opened her mouth to speak, but he stopped her. Placing his finger on her parted lips, he murmured, "If you apologize again, Amanda, I will be upset. I'm well beyond the teenage years of hormones running amok. I'm old enough to exert a little control over my libido."

She nodded and walked him to the door. He kissed her cheek. "I'll see you next week."

As she prepared for bed, Amanda could not help thinking how close they had come to making love. She had not planned to be sleeping alone that night. Every time he left with no more than a parting kiss, it had reminded her of the time following their marriage. She had to know if she had only imagined the desire, if it was just wishful thinking.

She had hoped her insistence on spending the afternoon and evening in would give him a hint as to what was on her mind. She had even considered the possibility that she might have to muster the courage to make the first move.

She felt guilty now because her strategy had worked. He had made his move, and then she proceeded to chicken out. Many men would have been upset and angry, but Drew had simply taken it in stride. She now knew that she had not imagined his desire.

She sighed. She had to let it go. The friendship they had established years earlier had not been destroyed during their separation. They had become even closer friends in the past few weeks. Once they overcame the initial strangeness, it was almost as if the intervening years had never happened. When the time was right, she would have no doubts about their relationship moving to the next logical step.

Four

The next week, Amanda was glad to see Friday arrive. It had been a hectic week and that day had been a particularly trying one. She had just undressed and was heading for the kitchen when the telephone interrupted her. She sighed. She was not in the mood for conversation, but when she heard Drew's voice on the machine, she picked up the receiver.

"Hi, sweetheart."

"Hi, Drew."

"How was your week?"

"Okay."

"Are you alright? You don't sound like yourself."

"I'm okay. It's been a rough day. I saw a child who'd been sexually abused."

"I'm sorry, Amanda."

"Thanks. Listen, Drew, about tomorrow. I don't think I'll be in any mood for company."

"Are you sure?"

"I'm sure."

After she hung up, Drew sat staring at the telephone. He did not like the sound of her voice. In spite of all she had been through in her life, it was unusual for her to sound so down.

He was also disturbed by the idea that she still thought of him as company. If nothing else, the previous week's events should have changed that definition. It was time he made it clear that he planned to be part of her life, not just an occasional visitor.

The following morning, Amanda had to drag herself out of bed. She had slept fitfully and felt no better than she had the previous evening. At eleven o'clock she had finished half a pot of coffee, but was still in her gown and robe. She knew she should start the laundry, or at least make her bed, but she could not seem to find the energy.

She had treated sexually abused children before, but it had never affected her this deeply. She knew the reason for that. She tried to convince herself that she was not to blame. She had not been entirely successful in assuaging her guilt.

Early that afternoon, there was a knock on the door. Amanda had not stirred from the position on the sofa that she had occupied since leaving her bed. Frowning, she went to see who was there. Seeing Drew's face through the peephole, she paused before opening the door.

Her distress was revealed in her eyes, and Drew was glad he had decided to ignore her suggestion that he cancel his visit. It was obvious she had not slept much the previous night. The fact that it was well after noon and she was not yet dressed was further evidence of her dejection.

"Hello, Amanda."

"Hi, Drew."

He raised his eyebrows in question when she made no move to invite him in. "May I come in?"

She stood aside, allowing him access. As he closed the door behind him, she asked, "What are you doing here? I thought we decided to cancel your visit this weekend."

"No, we didn't decide that. You said that you weren't

in the mood for company. Since I don't consider myself company, I decided that it didn't apply to me."

Amanda shook her head. "I didn't really mean company the way you refer to it. I guess what I really meant is that I'm not fit company to be around at the moment."

She returned to her seat on the sofa, and Drew followed her. After removing his jacket and laying it across the chair, he sat down beside her. Lifting her hand from her lap, he began gently stroking it.

"Do you want to talk about what has you so upset? Sometimes verbalizing the problem helps."

"That's supposed to be my line."

She took a deep breath. "There's not really much to tell. When I interviewed one of my patients yesterday, I learned that she's been suffering abuse from her uncle off and on for more than six months. He lived with the family for a few months until he moved to his own place about two months ago. While he lived there, and a few times after he moved out, he graciously offered to baby-sit. It was a perfect opportunity for him."

"Amanda, I'm sure you've dealt with this problem before. Does it always affect you this much?"

"It's something I'll never understand. She's only ten years old and her own uncle did this to her!" She closed her eyes. "But, no, it doesn't always affect me this deeply. This time was different, though. I've been seeing this child for other problems, including the depression she experienced after her grandmother's death. That was long before the abuse started. I should have noticed something different in her behavior when this problem arose."

"You can't blame yourself, sweetheart. You couldn't read the child's mind. She probably worked very hard at hiding what had happened. How did you find out what's been going on?"

"The truth came out yesterday. Her mother told me the child had recently had her first menstrual period and seemed upset about it. After some discussion, she finally admitted she was afraid of having a baby. At first I thought she believed getting her period meant she would get pregnant. I was upset that no one had explained the facts of life to her before now. Then the whole story came pouring out."

By now, tears were streaming down her face. Drew took her in his arms, pulling her onto his lap. He held her while she released all the frustration and anger.

After the discussions they had shared in the past few weeks, he had no doubt that she was dedicated to her patients, and a capable psychologist. He understood her anger at the man who had stolen a child's innocence, but she sounded as if she was also angry with herself. She was entitled to the former, but he was determined to make her see that she had no reason to be angry with herself.

Drew had long ago discovered that Amanda had a tendency to place too much blame on herself. It appeared she had not completely overcome that tendency, probably a holdover from her father's browbeating and constant criticism.

After a while, Amanda lifted her head from his shoulder and looked up at him. She had forgotten how good it felt being held in his arms.

"Feeling a little better?"

"I suppose."

"Amanda, I'll repeat what I said before. You can't blame yourself for this. Even though you've said there are usually signs indicating the possibility of abuse, the problem isn't that easy to detect."

He pulled a handkerchief from his pocket and wiped her tear-streaked face. "There's something else I have to say, and I hope you don't take this the wrong way. I'm sure you know more about this kind of thing than I do."

He looked away from her for a moment, hesitant to voice his opinion about her work. Amanda waited patiently for him to continue. Finally, he met her unwavering gaze.

"Don't you think it might be more worthwhile to set aside your regrets about not detecting the problem earlier and concentrate on what you can do to help the child now?"

"Drew, you're not telling me anything I haven't told myself. I promised myself years ago that I'd never be one of those people who wallows in self-pity. You're right. This isn't about me. It's about that little girl and helping her cope with what happened. I'm sure I'll get through this and be able to do that. I just get so disgusted and angry and frustrated every time I see it."

"I know, baby," he said, hugging her.

His hand stroked her back and Amanda was tempted to remain locked in his arms. When she recalled the previous fiasco, she decided she had to call a halt to his actions. She wanted him and she knew he wanted her, but desire was not enough. She had come to the conclusion that her need for more than that was what had stopped her a week earlier.

There had been no mention of love. She had struggled with that one-sided predicament six years ago. She had left then because she wanted more. She had wanted his love. She still wanted it. She had to know if his feelings had changed before she allowed herself to become any more deeply entangled in the relationship.

"I must really look a mess," she murmured, trying to smooth her disheveled hair.

"You could never look anything but beautiful to me."

"Thanks, but I think you're just trying to make me feel good."

She struggled to get up, but his arms tightened around her. Her heartbeat quickened when she looked in his eyes. The compassion that had been there earlier had changed to something very different. She had seen desire in his eyes before, but it had never been as intense as it was now. She took a deep breath.

"I think I've brooded long enough for one day."

"I think you're entitled to a little brooding. Of course, just because you've decided not to mope any longer doesn't mean you have to move from here. I could get used to this."

"I need to take a shower and get dressed, Drew."

He sighed and loosened his hold. "If you insist."

She stood up and moved away from the sofa. Putting more space between them helped restore her composure. Her mood had also improved considerably. His mere presence had that effect on her.

"I don't suppose I have to tell you to make yourself at home." She started toward the bedroom, smiling. "In fact," she added over her shoulder, "since you've already told me you're not company, feel free to start cleaning. I didn't get around to it this morning. The vacuum cleaner is in the hall closet."

Drew chuckled as she walked away. He felt good knowing that her spirits had been restored.

A short time later, Amanda stepped from the shower. As she wrapped the towel around her body, she frowned. Straining her ears, she could not believe the sound coming from the living room.

After making her bed, she dressed and returned to the living room. There was no sign of Drew, but she took notice of the freshly vacuumed floor and newly polished furniture.

The sounds coming from the kitchen drew her attention and she went to investigate. Drew had loaded the dishwasher and was wiping the counters.

She stopped in the doorway. She leaned against the frame, her arms crossed over her chest.

"Can you hold that pose long enough for me to load my camera? This is definitely one of those Kodak moments. Too bad I don't own an apron."

He turned from his task, smiling. "Are you hinting that I'm a male chauvinist?"

"Not really. As I recall, I can't honestly accuse you of that."

He set the sponge on the back of the sink and came toward her. His gaze locked with hers. He was only a few inches away when he reached out and caressed her cheek.

"I'm glad you remember some of the good things about our time together."

She remembered everything about their time together and to her, it was all good. The only problem had been the fact that he was not in love with her. In all fairness, she could not hold that against him. She could only hope that his feelings would change.

His touch had the effect of weaving a spell. The desire she had glimpsed in his eyes earlier now enveloped them both. Amanda could not tear her eyes from his. Her voice seemed to have deserted her. Even if she had managed to speak, she could think of nothing to say without revealing her thoughts.

The ringing of the telephone broke the spell. With

some effort, she tore her gaze from his. She excused herself and went to answer the phone.

Drew watched her cross the room. In his mind he compared this graceful, confident woman to the teenager he had fallen in love with. Although she had never shown a lack of self-esteem, there was a difference in her now. She had gained a new self-assurance that had been lacking in her immaturity.

Within a few minutes, she finished her telephone call and returned to the kitchen. "That was my director of the counseling center. She was worried about me. I guess when I left yesterday I wasn't as controlled as I thought."

Just then her stomach sent out a loud protest. For the first time, she realized she had eaten nothing since lunch the previous day.

"I think your stomach just decided the next order of business. Where do you want to go for lunch?"

"We don't have to go anywhere. I'll fix some sandwiches."

"Only if you promise to let me take you out to dinner this evening."

Drew watched her closely while she fixed the sandwiches and later as they ate. She had regained her equilibrium, but he did not make the mistake of thinking she had totally recovered from her anxiety over the child. He had no doubt she would get over it eventually. She had an innate strength. She would never have survived life with her father without it.

Before long, she began talking about the child who was at the center of her turmoil. Drew let her talk, asking a few encouraging questions. After a while, she took a deep breath.

"I guess I was rambling."

"That's okay. You needed to get it out of your system. The importance of verbalizing the problem, remember."

After lunch, they settled on the sofa again. She turned on the television and Drew became engrossed in the football game. During one of the breaks, he noticed that she was trying very hard not to yawn, and looked as if she might nod off to sleep any minute.

"Amanda, we've already established the fact that I'm not company. I won't be insulted if you want to take a nap."

"I'm okay."

He reached over and pulled her closer. "You're not okay. You probably had very little sleep last night. At least lay your head down and rest."

She was too drowsy to understand what he was actually suggesting until he urged her head down on the pillow in his lap. She stretched her legs out on the sofa and, within minutes, she was sound asleep.

Drew was perfectly content to sit there watching her. One of his arms lay across her waist and periodically, his other hand would brush her hair back from her face when she stirred in her sleep.

Amanda slept for more than two hours. When she opened her eyes it was to find that, in addition to her head being on his lap, her hand rested familiarly on his thigh. Drew's arm lay across her waist and the football game had ended.

She could easily become accustomed to such a cozy arrangement, but more than a few moments' indulgence in that fantasy could be dangerous. She stirred and lifted his hand from her waist.

Drew helped her to a sitting position as she brushed her hair back from her face. "I know we decided you aren't company, but I can't help feeling I've been extremely rude for falling asleep on you," she murmured, stretching.

Drew's immediate thought was to wish her statement was literal. He momentarily envisioned her lying naked on top of him. He wisely forced that picture from his mind.

"That nap is probably just what you needed. I'd hate to have to pull your head out of your plate in the middle of dinner."

"I'll ignore that remark. I don't think I was that far gone."

Drew chuckled and leaned over, planting a kiss on the tip of her nose. "Where would you like to go for dinner?"

"It doesn't matter. There's a little steakhouse not far from here."

They had an early dinner at the restaurant she recommended. She was surprised and a little disappointed when Drew suggested a movie after dinner. She had hoped to spend a quiet evening in her apartment. She wondered if her actions the previous week were responsible for his reluctance to spend more time alone with her there.

Drew's suggestion was based more on his own feelings than Amanda's actions. It had only been a week since she had drawn away from his advances. He was determined to give her more time to be sure she wanted him as much as he wanted her. He admitted to himself that his motives were not entirely altruistic. He was not ready to cope with another rejection.

It was late when they returned to her apartment. Drew entered the apartment with her, but did not remove his jacket. When she turned to face him, her disappointment was evident. There was no sign of the distress he had seen earlier that day.

"Are you sure you're alright?"

Amanda nodded. "I'll be fine."

Drew fought the urge to give in to his own desire and the desire he read in her eyes. They gazed at each other for a long moment. Unspoken words hung in the air. Neither of them would acknowledge the passion simmering below the surface.

Drew kissed her tenderly, and much too briefly. "I'll call you tomorrow."

A moment later, he was gone and Amanda was left staring at the door. She fought the temptation to call him back, to tell him that she wanted him to stay and make love to her. She shook her head absently, to clear it of the dangerous thoughts and visions running through her mind. After turning out the lights, she made her way to her bedroom.

Two more weeks of the same routine followed. Drew visited each weekend, and they spent the afternoon watching football. At first, he expressed guilt over spending their time together watching television, but Amanda assured him that it was perfectly acceptable. She was beginning to enjoy the games herself. Or maybe the truth was she would enjoy any pastime, as long as they were together.

She did wonder if his absorption in football was his way of avoiding a possibility of a romantic interlude. Maybe he was upset over her rejecting his advances, even though he had insisted otherwise. On the other hand, he showed no inclination to stop his weekly visits or his frequent telephone calls. She reminded herself of her own misgivings and her determination to win his love. She had to be patient.

Five

By late October, Amanda was seriously questioning whether she had misread Drew's desire. He had made no further attempt to make love to her. She thought about the only time he had tried, and she refused to believe she had turned him off completely with that one rejection.

She had to admit that she had been confused about her own feelings. How could she blame him for being hesitant when she had been giving mixed signals? She wanted him, but she also wanted his love.

When he called near the end of that month suggesting dinner Friday evening, she was surprised. In the past, he never arrived before Saturday.

Amanda spent an inordinate amount of time deciding on an outfit. She finally settled on a burgundy wool crepe A-line dress with a cowl neck. A silver pin with matching earrings, along with gray suede pumps and clutch, completed the outfit.

Dinner was a romantic candlelit affair, a departure from their previous dates. Although Drew had visited her a number of times and each time they had gone out to dinner, this occasion was different.

The ambience of the restaurant itself was different from most of the others they had frequented. There was more to it than that, though. The aura that surrounded them was due more to their underlying emotions than the external decor of the restaurant. The spoken topics of conversation were general; it was the unspoken conversation that was disquieting. Whenever their gazes met, which was often, she felt a distinct warmth spreading through her body.

They had almost finished their meal when Drew broached the subject that had been on his mind for years. "There's something I need to know, Amanda. The note you left years ago explained your reasons for leaving, but I couldn't help thinking there was more to it. I need to know if it was something I did that made you run away."

Amanda's eyes widened. She frowned. How could he think that he had done something wrong? She had to ease his mind, but she could not tell him the whole truth, not yet. She shook her head.

"No, Drew, you weren't the cause of my leaving. You were always very kind to me. I just came to the conclusion that I had to learn to make it on my own. For lack of a better phrase, I needed to find myself. I know that term has been overworked. What it meant for me is that I had to stop hiding behind you."

"So in a way, it was my fault."

"If being too kind is a fault, I suppose you could say that. I can't use that as an excuse, though. Believe me, Drew, the problem was with me, not you.

"Since this seems to be a question-and-answer session, I've been wondering about a few things myself. I remember what you said about wanting to help me get away from my father, but there had to have been more to it than that. You didn't believe me when I said I wasn't pregnant and yet you were willing to marry me, thinking I was carrying another man's child. Why?"

Drew shrugged. He thought back to that time and his motivations.

"From the discussion in my office, I assumed the child's father was out of the picture, for whatever reason. I didn't really care about the reason. He was unimportant. I was more concerned about your welfare. I knew your life and the child's would be a living nightmare if you kept the child and continued to live with your father.

"I liked you and I admired you for a number of reasons. In the time that you worked in our office I had seen examples of your intelligence for myself, and Betty was always singing your praises. Even before that day, she had hinted of the problems with your father. I couldn't let your potential go to waste knowing I had it in my power to do something about it."

She remembered his father's secretary, Betty. She had supervised Amanda and always insisted on hearing about her schoolwork and her grades.

Drew continued with his list. "I admired your courage and strength, your refusal to give up in spite of your father's abuse."

He smiled. "I liked your sense of humor, too. I didn't see much of that, but I never forgot what you said after your appendix surgery."

His smile faded. He remembered the panic he felt the day he arrived home and found her collapsed in pain on the living room floor. Even after he rushed her to the hospital, the fear had not subsided. That episode was the first inkling he had of his feelings for her. He was forced to admit to himself that he was motivated by more than general concern.

She looked puzzled at his statement. She had been so groggy, she had no idea what she said to him.

He smiled again. "You told me to tell your father you gave birth to a rotten appendix."

"I don't remember that. I do remember your apology for not believing me."

They fell silent, recalling those days years ago. There was more that Drew wanted to tell her, but he was still unsure of the reaction he could expect to a confession of love. He had reason to believe she shared his passion, but did her feelings go any deeper than that?

Amanda mulled over his words. He talked about admiration and she had seen the desire in his eyes, but there was still no mention of love.

When they returned to her apartment, she invited him in. Although the evening had been a departure from his usual Saturday visit, she expected he would make some excuse and leave. He had given no reason for changing their date to Friday. It occurred to her that he might have to work the next day. Instead of making his excuses and leaving, he nodded acceptance. He took the key from her hand, sending a prickle of awareness and anticipation through her body.

When they entered the living room, Amanda stepped out of her shoes and settled on the sofa, curling her legs up under her. She was no longer a naive teenager, and she could guess where the evening would end. She was more than willing to accept that conclusion; she was almost hoping for it. As much as she wanted him, though, she had to have more answers first. She hesitated, not sure where to start.

Drew sat down beside her, looking at her intently. "What's on your mind, Amanda? You look like you have more questions."

"Yes, I do. I'm not sure this is the right time to bring it up, but I have to know. At the restaurant, you explained your reasons for marrying me. I admit your explanation didn't surprise me."

She looked down and began smoothing her dress. Saying what she had on her mind was impossible to do while staring into those ebony depths.

"At the time you married me, you gave me the impression that you really thought of me more as a sister than a wife. Your actions, or inaction, reinforced that idea. Even to the point of giving me a separate bedroom. You waited months before you gave me any indication that you wanted a physical relationship. Even when you made love to me, it was like you didn't really want to, you just thought you should."

Drew took a deep breath. "I'll be honest with you, Amanda. I didn't think of you exactly as a sister— more as a friend. After living with you for a while, I realized that my feelings for you had changed. Friendship wasn't enough."

He paused, remembering that first tentative overture. It was the Valentine's Day a few months after her recovery from appendicitis.

"Amanda, when I made love to you it was because I couldn't resist it any longer. I'd wanted you for months. Believe me, the hesitancy you sensed was not because I didn't want you, but because I felt guilty."

"Guilty? Why should you feel guilty? I was your wife."

"When we got married you were so young, just seventeen years old."

Amanda smiled. "Drew, I was almost eighteen. Besides, there are a number of seventeen-year-olds out there with children."

"I know, but you were different. You seemed so innocent. There was also the idea that you might not feel you had a choice. I finally realized that if we were to have a real marriage, it had to be a marriage in every sense of the word.''

"But you still felt guilty.''

Drew shrugged. He hesitated to tell her that his guilt was partly due to her own actions.

"Drew?''

"You said you sensed that I made love to you because I thought I should. That's what I thought about you. I thought you allowed me to make love to you because you thought it was what you were supposed to do.''

She wanted to tell him she had been waiting, hoping he would make love to her. She opened her mouth to say just that, but he went on.

"In fact, I thought it was part of the reason you left.''

"How could you think I'd leave because of that? It wasn't as if you forced me. In fact, as I recall, you were very patient and gentle.''

"I tried to be. I don't think it was very enjoyable for you, though.''

"I didn't have any experience then, but I never believed everything I read in novels. I also learned that, in spite of what some books and some people would have us believe, the reality is usually quite different. I'm sure it's not uncommon for the first few times to be less than spectacular. You're wrong, though. It was very enjoyable for me.''

He reached over, took her hand, and lifted it to his lips. It was time to lay all the cards on the table.

"You don't know how glad I am to hear that. When I came home that day and found your note, I wanted to kick myself. That was when I realized that somewhere along the way I had fallen in love with you.''

Amanda shook her head and gently pulled her hand away. There, he had said the words she had been waiting to hear. Now, perversely, she had difficulty believing him.

"Don't say that, Drew. You said you were going to be honest. If you loved me, why didn't you come after me? You've already said you knew where I was living."

"There were a few reasons. You told me in your note that you needed to make it on your own. As concerned as I was about your welfare, I had no right to try to take that chance from you."

His thumb caressed the knuckles of her hand. "There was another reason, too. On one hand, you might have agreed to come back just because you thought you owed it to me. I didn't want that. On the other hand, I didn't relish the possibility of rejection. I had no idea what you felt, other than gratitude."

She reached over and touched his cheek. "I can't believe you actually thought I'd turn you away," she murmured. "I've been in love with you since I was sixteen years old."

The words had barely left her mouth before he pulled her onto his lap and into his arms. His mouth came down on hers just seconds after she recognized the desire blazing in his eyes. She reached up, twining her arms around his neck and leaning into the hard muscles of his chest.

Drew's arms tightened, pulling her closer. One hand slid up to cup the enticing globe that had been tempting him all evening. She tasted so good, so sweet. The scent of her perfume permeated the air, fueling the embers that had been smoldering since that afternoon. When his thumb grazed over the nipple, it hardened immediately.

"I want another chance, Amanda. I want to show you just how spectacular it can be."

Amanda could barely force the words from her

lips. "I want it too, Drew. There's just one thing more, though. It won't matter if it's not spectacular."

Within moments they were in her bedroom. He unzipped her dress and pushed it from her shoulders. She stepped out of it, but before she could pick it up, he had retrieved it and tossed it on a nearby chair. Seconds later, he had likewise disposed of her remaining garments.

Amanda reached out with trembling hands and unbuttoned his shirt, pulling it from his slacks. He shrugged out of it as her fingers loosened his slacks and reached for the zipper. Her hands stopped abruptly in their quest when his finger began trailing a pattern across her collarbone and down between her breasts. She gasped and clutched his shoulders.

He completed the task and drew her to him. She shivered in his arms, the sensation of warm skin next to warm skin more sensuous than she remembered. His scent enveloped her while his hands stroked her skin, igniting a fire that spread through her body.

After pulling back the covers, Drew gently laid her on the bed. His hands continued to work their magic as his mouth claimed hers once again. This time there was no teasing; all the pent-up hunger was unleashed. Her response made it clear that she shared his appetite, which fed his own passion.

"Please, Drew."

Within moments, they were locked in the ancient dance of love. Her hands splayed across his back and then lower, kneading the flexing muscles of his buttocks. Drew moaned when she wrapped her legs around his waist, urging him deeper into the wet sheath. He managed to insinuate his fingers between their bodies, finding the hard nub that had become the center of her being. Her shivers of ecstasy were the impetus that sent him over the edge. Minutes later, their passion sated, they were sound asleep, locked in each other's arms.

Amanda was the first to awaken. Propping herself on her elbow, she lay staring at his profile. She recalled telling him that their lovemaking in the past had been enjoyable, if not spectacular. Afraid of expecting too much, she had convinced herself that mildly pleasurable would be enough. It had been years since their first few times, but the previous night had definitely been closer to spectacular than merely enjoyable.

She stretched and eased from the bed, unaware that her movement had awakened Drew. He was fascinated by the sensuous movement of her nude body. He assumed that she was headed for the shower and fought the temptation to join her. Instead, he fluffed the pillows behind him and settled down to await her return.

Fifteen minutes later, she exited the bathroom clad in a terry cloth robe that hid the curves he had thoroughly explored the previous night. Amanda came to an abrupt halt when she entered the bedroom. She opened her mouth to speak, but the words caught in her throat when he threw back the covers and rose from the bed.

His nude body reminded her of the passion they had shared. Her hand itched to feel again those hard muscles flexing beneath her fingers. She pulled her attention from his body and started across the room, but he intercepted her.

"Good morning," he murmured, leaning over to plant a kiss on her cheek.

She swallowed hard and finally managed to find

her voice. "Good morning. I'm finished in the bath-room. There are linens in the hall closet."

"You wouldn't happen to have an extra tooth-brush, would you?"

"I think there's one in the vanity drawer."

Amanda took a deep breath as the bathroom door closed behind him. Not stopping to dress, she headed for the kitchen to start breakfast. She had just poured herself a cup of coffee when Drew joined her in the kitchen.

"Do you want coffee?"

"I'll get it," he insisted.

"What would you like for breakfast? There's not a lot to choose from. I have cereal and eggs and juice."

"Eggs and toast will be fine, but I can cook it my-self."

"I don't mind. I'll do it. Actually, I can do a little better than plain eggs," she added, looking in the refrigerator. "How about a cheese omelet?"

"That sounds good."

They ate in relative silence. Drew complimented the meal and brushed aside her apology for not having anything more substantial in the house. Neither spoke of the passion that still simmered below the surface.

When they finished eating, he rose from his chair and walked over to the counter. Returning with the coffeepot, he refilled both their cups and carried the pot back to the counter. The simple activity gave him time to consider his next words. He was wary that she might feel he was rushing her into a permanent ar-rangement.

"Amanda, I think we have some important things to discuss," he said, slowly stirring his coffee.

"Yes, I suppose we do. Where do we start?"

He reached over and lifted her hand from the table. Shivers traveled up her arm when he planted a kiss in the palm.

"Well, I guess you could say last night was actually the start. Logically, the next step would be for us to move in together. How do you feel about that?"

For a brief moment, Amanda imagined another forty or fifty years of the passion that was still fresh in her mind. It was much more than that, though. She remembered his compassion and tenderness. She remembered feeling totally content when she slept peacefully with her head in his lap.

"Amanda? Do you have a problem with taking that step?"

She forced her attention back to the question at hand. "No, Drew. It's just that there are a few complications that would have to be ironed out. For one thing, moving in together obviously means I would be the one relocating. That, in turn, means I'd have to leave my job."

"I guess it seems a little chauvinistic, but I think that plan would be more feasible since my business is already established in Philadelphia."

"I don't think it's chauvinistic, just realistic. It'll be easier for me to find work in one of the agencies in Philadelphia than for you to relocate your business, and probably lose some clients. I just hate to leave the children who've come to know me and trust me."

He nodded. He had seen an example of her attachment to her patients.

"I understand. I imagine it's impossible not to form attachments in your profession. Unfortunately, I can't think of another solution. Commuting doesn't appear to be a practical option."

"I agree that commuting isn't feasible. Relocating won't be that simple, though. It'll be a while before

I can make all the arrangements, possibly more than a few weeks. I'll have to give Sharon time to find a replacement. And you're right about forming attachments. I need time to prepare the children."

And myself, she thought. She loved him and she believed he loved her, but making the reconciliation official was a big step.

"Since you're making the biggest concession, it would be very selfish of me to complain about a little delay. It's enough for now to know that you feel the same as I do. I've waited more than six years for us to be together. I can wait a few more months if I have to. That is, as long as we can still have our weekends together."

Amanda rose from her chair and came to stand directly in front of him. Drew wrapped his arms around her waist. She placed her hands on his shoulders as he pulled her onto his lap. Sliding her fingers beneath the fabric of his shirt, she began teasing the sprinkling of hairs on his chest.

"Does that mean you won't be rushing back to Philadelphia every Saturday?"

Drew chuckled, loosening the tie belt to her robe. His hand captured one breast, gently kneading it.

"Believe me, I plan to be here every weekend, for the entire weekend. In fact, you may have to kick me out on Monday morning."

Amanda gasped when his tongue replaced his fingers, laving the taut peak, while his hand moved to explore new territory. She moaned his name when his fingers found the soft, moist place between her thighs. Before she could regain her senses, he had set her on her feet and stripped off his own clothes. He then relieved her of her robe.

She was caught off guard for a moment when he urged her onto his lap, straddling his thighs. His tongue resumed its pleasant torture as he entered her hot, wet sheath. It was his turn to moan when her body tightened around his swollen member. His hands clasping her waist, he guided her into the rhythm that soon drove them over the edge. When she collapsed against him, he tightened his arms around her, stroking her soft, silky skin.

A few minutes later, Amanda lifted her head from his chest. She brushed her hair back from her face. Her breathing and pulse rate had almost returned to normal until she looked up and met his gaze.

Drew took her face in his hands, planting a soft warm kiss on her lips. "I can't believe you're here in my arms. I've dreamed of this for so long. I love you, Amanda."

He looked so serious. Her thumb stroked his bottom lip before she kissed him tenderly.

"I love you, too. I never meant to hurt you, Drew."

"I know that, sweetheart. What happened six years ago doesn't matter now. All that matters is that we're together again."

Amanda squirmed and he groaned. "Speaking of together, I think we'd better get up or we may be here for the rest of the day."

Six

Drew convinced her to return to Philadelphia with him that evening. When he arrived on Friday, he had been hesitant to raise his expectations of spending the night. He was totally unprepared to spend the entire weekend. The only clothes he had with him were those on his back.

That wasn't his only reason for asking her to come home with him. He was eager for her to again see the house. In the years since her absence, he had made quite a few changes. He had purchased it about eight months before their marriage at an amazingly reasonable price because of the repairs needed.

Amanda stepped into the large entry hall and stared around at the beige shadow striped wallpaper and dark oak stained woodwork. An Oriental runner in red, navy, and gold carpeted the semicircular oak staircase slightly to the left of the door. A medium-size round table sat on top of a matching circular carpet in the center of the hallway.

Drew set her bag down in the hall and took her hand. "The repairs have been completed since you were here, but there's still a lot of decorating to be done. If I remember correctly, you enjoyed doing that. Maybe that's why I was never in a great hurry to finish that job."

He led her across the hall to the right, into the living room that extended the entire length of the house. The huge carpeted room was divided into two separate areas. The section closest to the front of the house was a cozy conversation area with a beautiful marble fireplace. At the other end of the room was a grand piano and several chairs.

"I found the piano at an auction. I couldn't resist it. It needed some work, but I've had it completely restored."

"Don't you think it's a rather large conversation piece? You don't play the piano, do you?"

"No, I don't, but I remember you saying that you had taken lessons for a couple of years before your mother died. I had the impression you would like to continue them some day."

He loosened his hold on her hand and she strolled slowly across the room. Drew followed, watching her intently. Tears formed in her eyes as she lovingly stroked the beautiful old instrument. She turned and looked at him, shaking her head in wonder.

"I don't know what to say, Drew. It's beautiful."

"I'm glad you like it."

She closed the short space between them and hugged him. "Thank you."

"You're welcome," he murmured, kissing the top of her head. "You realize, of course, that this means you can't renege on your plans to take lessons."

She looked up at him, smiling. "Does that mean you'll be standing over me with a ruler to make sure I practice?"

He chuckled and nodded. "If absolutely necessary." He kissed her cheek. "Shall we finish the tour?"

A door to the right of the living room led to a combination office/library. The house was magnificent.

Although it had needed a lot of work when she left, she had seen its potential. He had maintained the original oak mouldings and woodwork throughout. The carpeted dining room to the right of the entrance hall was empty except for a large mirror and sconces on the wall.

"Since I never did much entertaining, I didn't consider this room a priority," he explained.

The kitchen had been completely gutted and redone with dark oak cabinets and every possible convenience. A small breakfast area off from the kitchen opened to the deck that extended the entire back width of the house.

Upstairs, only two of the five bedrooms were completely furnished. The house had originally included six bedrooms, but two of them had been combined into a huge master suite. Two walk-in closets flanked the master bathroom with its whirlpool tub and double-size shower.

A large portion of the remodeling had been done when she lived with him, but the bathroom and the furniture were new. She was a little surprised at the huge four-poster oak bed. She thought the four-poster style would be too feminine for most men's taste, although the four-inch-thick spiral posts could hardly be considered feminine.

A brick fireplace added to the romantic ambience. Amanda was not sure if it was the room or her memory of recent events that were responsible for the warmth that crept through her body.

She was so preoccupied with those memories that Drew called her name twice before she turned her attention to him. He had placed her overnight bag on the bed and was gesturing to one of the closets.

"There's plenty of room in here. I'll switch all my clothes to the other closet before you move in."

He walked over to her and took both her hands in his. She looked up at him expectantly.

"You have no idea how good it feels to say those words."

Drew had noticed her gazing at the bed. He took a deep breath. "There's something I have to tell you, Amanda. I won't lie and try to convince you that I've been celibate for the past six years. I will tell you that there've been very few women in my life since you left."

He gestured toward the bed. "I don't know if it will mean anything to you, but I want you to know that no other woman has ever shared this bed with me. Strangely enough, that wasn't even a conscious decision. In the back of my mind, I was convinced that some day we'd be together again. I guess I wanted to save this room for that day."

He shrugged. "That probably sounds more than a little odd, maybe even unbelievable."

Amanda leaned up and kissed his cheek. "Maybe to someone else. I thinks it's very special and very believable, coming from a man who bought a beautiful grand piano on the basis of a girl's hope to someday continue her lessons. You've always been honest with me Drew, sometimes painfully so. I have no reason to think that's changed."

Drew smiled down at her. "I think I'd better go see about dinner. If I stay here, we'll be putting that bed to use now. And once I get you in that bed, I might not let you out of it until tomorrow."

They had nearly finished their meal when an unpleasant thought occurred to Amanda. "Drew, in the past few weeks I think we've discussed most of the obstacles that stood in our way before. There is one problem I haven't mentioned in our other discussions, though."

"What is it?"

"Your parents. They won't be any happier this time than they were the first. In fact, it will probably be even worse. I'm sure when you married me, they realized it wasn't because you were madly in love."

"That was probably the real reason they were so much against it."

Amanda shook her head. "I don't think so, Drew."

He took her hand. "It doesn't matter what they think, Amanda. I love you. I've loved you for years. I plan to spend the rest of my life with you."

Amanda gave up. There was no way she could explain. How could she tell him that his mother was a mean and spiteful woman? The older woman had always been careful to save her more vicious remarks until the two of them were alone. Whatever his mother's reaction might be when she learned of their reconciliation, Amanda would handle it. It was different now. She was different. She knew Drew loved her, and she was no longer an insecure teenager.

The weekend passed much too swiftly. All too soon, Monday morning arrived. Drew had left the previous evening, after seeing her home.

When she arrived at the center, Amanda's first order of business was to inform the director that she would be leaving in a few months.

"Is everything alright, Amanda? I know you were upset about Maya."

Amanda nodded. She admitted to herself that when she told Drew of her determination to prepare the children for her leaving, Maya had been uppermost in her mind. She was not so egotistical as to think that no other psychologist was capable of treating the child. She just had to assure herself that Maya was well on her way to recovery before she resigned from the center.

"I was upset, Sharon, but that's not why I'm leaving. I'm getting married." She had already decided that the truth was too complicated to explain.

"Congratulations! When's the date?"

"We haven't set a specific date yet. I can't leave until I feel comfortable that Maya is going to get through this awful situation."

"Amanda, I know how dedicated you are to your patients, but it wouldn't be fair to you or your fiancé to postpone the wedding. I'm sure one of the other therapists could take over."

"We're not planning a big wedding and I'm not really postponing it. I couldn't leave without giving you plenty of notice. Drew understands that. I'll start preparing Maya and the other children."

"It might be a good idea for me to sit in on some of your sessions, if you have no objections. I'll wait a week or so, until you've had time to explain to them that you'll be leaving. I have your reports, but seeing their responses and progress firsthand will help make the transition smoother."

"Of course I don't have any objections, Sharon. I think it's a good idea."

On Thursday evening, Amanda decided she could no longer put off telling Nicole the news. Even though her friend had been responsible for keeping Drew informed of Amanda's activities over the years, she could not be certain of Nicole's reaction to their reconciliation.

She had only spoken with Nicole twice since the wedding. She had not mentioned the fact that she and Drew had agreed to give their relationship another chance. She supposed that somewhere in the back of her mind was the idea that voicing her hopes might jinx them. Her neglect to discuss this with her friend was the reason why she was now hesitant to reveal the latest development.

She dialed the number and the two women chatted for a few minutes before Amanda explained the real reason for the call. "Drew and I are getting back together."

Nicole's response was slow. "Just what does getting back together mean? You're dating again?"

"Well, actually, we've been dating for a while now, since the wedding."

"Then I guess 'getting back together' means you're moving in with him."

Amanda cleared her throat. "Sort of."

Nicole finally put the pieces together. "You're getting married again? When did all this come about?"

"That's the other piece of news. We're already married. Drew never got a divorce."

"Whoa, girlfriend. You've been holding out on me. How long have you known?"

"Since your wedding. When he told me about the divorce, or rather, the fact that there was no divorce, he suggested we start dating. Last weekend we . . . well, we decided to give the marriage another chance. I love him, Nicole. You know I've always loved him. And he loves me, he really loves me."

"I know, Amanda."

"What do you mean, you know?"

"Okay, I didn't know, but I've had strong suspicions. The day you left, I called your house, looking for you. Drew answered, and when he told me you had left, there was something in his voice that started me thinking. He said he was just concerned about your welfare, but he sounded too upset for that to be all there was to it."

Nicole paused, considering the can of worms she might be opening. "If you've been dating since my wedding, I'm sure he's told you I've kept him up to date on your life."

"Yes, he told me."

"And?"

"And what?"

"Are you angry? I had to let him know you were alright, Amanda. I couldn't just ignore his questions, Amanda. He was so worried about you."

"You don't have to explain, Nicole. I'm not angry."

"I'm really happy for you, Amanda. After seeing you two at my wedding, I knew you belonged together."

"Thanks, Nicole, for everything. I have another favor to ask. We're still married, but after six years' separation, we decided that a renewal of our vows is in order. We're not having a big wedding or anything, but I'd like for you to be there."

"You know I will. When's the ceremony?"

"We don't know yet. I have to tie up some loose ends here, so it probably won't be for a few months. I'll let you know as soon as we set a date."

The next few weeks were hectic for Amanda. She put in extra time with some of her patients, especially Maya. The girl was improving, but Amanda knew it would be a while before she was ready to be discharged from regular counseling sessions. She had taken the news of Amanda's departure well. Amanda had promised the child's mother that she would be available to help if Maya later felt the need to talk to her.

In mid-November, Nicole called Amanda to invite her for Thanksgiving dinner. "I don't know if you and Drew have other plans, but David and I would love to have you over."

"Drew hasn't mentioned any other plans. I assumed he would be having dinner with his family, in which case I might take you up on your invitation for myself."

"Don't you think, under the circumstances, he'd expect you to go with him?"

"I was trying not to think about that possibility."

"Amanda, you can't ignore that situation forever. You'll have to face them sooner or later."

"Hopefully, it'll be later. I'll see Drew this weekend and I'll let you know about Thanksgiving."

Amanda would have been even more upset if she were aware of the conversation Drew had with his parents that same week. He decided it was time to inform them that he and Amanda had reconciled.

"What do you mean, you're getting back together with her? You can't be serious. You're actually going to marry that girl, again?"

Drew cleared his throat. His mother's reaction was not totally unexpected, but he had hoped she would mellow over the years.

"Her name is Amanda, Mom, and the truth is we're already married. We do plan to renew our vows, though, and I'd like you and Dad to be there."

Claire's mouth dropped open. "Are you telling me that in the six years you've been separated, you never filed for divorce? I can't believe this! I'm certainly glad I urged you to have her sign that prenuptial agreement years ago. You do still have it, don't you?"

Drew shook his head. He recalled Amanda's insistence on replacing the money she had taken from the bank account. Of course, he could never give his mother that information. She would latch onto the fact that Amanda had taken the money and hear nothing beyond that.

Claire misread the look on her son's face. Evidently,

he had seen no need to keep that important document.

"You mean you destroyed it when she left? Well, you'll just have to have her sign another one before you reconcile. That could present another problem, though. If she learns that you destroyed the first one, she might use that against you."

Claire was outraged when Drew laughed at her suggestion. "I see nothing amusing about this situation, Andrew."

Drew knew she was displeased with his reaction. She only called him by his full name when she was upset with him.

"Mom, that suggestion was even more unnecessary six years ago than it is now. You act as if I had millions of dollars and Amanda was an experienced gold digger. She was an innocent, naive teenager when I married her."

"What are you trying to tell me?"

"I'm telling you I never asked Amanda to sign a prenuptial agreement. There's no way I could have put her through that. As for now, the reconciliation was my idea. I pursued her. I'm in love with her. I've been in love with her for years. Why can't you understand and accept that?"

She shook her head. "She played on your sympathy years ago and you fell for it. I can't believe you're still that gullible. I think you're mistaking sympathy for love."

Drew stifled the anger that threatened to explode. "I give up. Maybe when you get to know her, you'll see what a wonderful, generous, loving person she is."

Claire threw up her hands. "Well, you're an adult. If you insist on doing this, that's your decision, but I can't be a party to it."

Before he left his parents' home, Drew's mother issued her invitation for Thanksgiving. She did not refuse to allow Amanda to join them, but it was obvious she was not happy about it.

"I'm sorry, Mom, I won't be here for Thanksgiving this year. We've made other plans."

He knew nothing of Nicole's invitation, but he had no intention of subjecting Amanda to his mother's animosity at this early stage in their relationship. They would probably join his family for Christmas dinner. He suspected that it would not be a pleasant occasion for Amanda, and to ask her to cope with such a gathering twice within a month's time was too much. He hoped his mother would learn to accept Amanda when she realized that he planned to spend the rest of his life with her.

His father walked him to the door. The older man had observed closely the exchange between Drew and his mother. He felt compelled to offer an explanation for his silence.

"Drew, I'm sorry. I have to admit that, originally, I shared your mother's opposition to your marriage. I finally accepted your right to make your own choice. I also recognized that you could have done much worse in choosing a wife. My main concern was Amanda's age. That's no longer an issue. If you really love each other, you owe it to yourselves to give the marriage another chance."

He sighed. "I've lived with your mother for almost thirty-five years. I tried to talk her out of her opposition to Amanda years ago, but she wouldn't budge then and she's too stubborn to change her opinion now. I won't openly oppose her, but I won't continue to go along with her choice. Let me know when you've made the arrangements. I'll be there for the ceremony."

Drew hugged his father. "Thanks, Dad. I really appreciate that."

Seven

When Amanda informed Drew of Nicole's invitation, he readily agreed. He had arrived that evening for the weekend and they were in the middle of dinner.

"I have to admit I'm a little surprised that you aren't planning to have dinner with your parents."

Drew shrugged. "We don't always have Thanksgiving together. There've been a few years when they were out of town."

Amanda looked down at her plate. "Did they invite you this year, Drew? Have you told them about us?"

He reached over and took her hand in his. "You won't let it go, will you? Yes, I've told them about us and we were invited for Thanksgiving dinner."

"In that case, your mother must have made it clear that she wasn't thrilled about including me."

The look on his face told her the truth. It also told her that he was upset about it.

"Drew, it's okay. Don't let it upset you. I'm used to your mother's attitude. I didn't expect it to change. I'm a big girl now. I can handle it."

"Well, on the bright side, I can tell you that her attitude isn't shared by my father. You already know how my sister Jennifer feels about you. I'm sure that eventually, my mother will come around."

"If she does, fine. If not, I'll have to learn to live with it. I love you, Drew. She can't change that and I won't let her destroy our happiness."

The day before Thanksgiving, Amanda drove to Philadelphia. She arrived at Drew's house just in time for dinner. He helped her off with her coat and hung it in the closet.

"I was beginning to get worried. I called your place twice."

"I guess I should have called. I was a little late leaving the center. I had a report I wanted to finish since I won't be returning to the office until Monday."

He took her garment bag and they started up the stairs. "How are things going at the center? Have they decided to hire a replacement for you?"

"That's the plan, not that they have much choice. Sharon's interviewed a few people, but she hasn't made a choice yet."

They entered the bedroom and he placed her case on the bed. "I think you have time to unpack, but don't take too long. Dinner's almost ready." He planted a kiss on her cheek and left her to her task.

Amanda joined him in the kitchen a short time later. "It smells good in here. What are we having?"

"Good old-fashioned beef stew. I decided the weather called for something hearty. I can't believe how cold it is out there already. Originally, I thought it would be a good way to warm you up."

He crossed the room and took her in his arms. "The more I thought about it, though, I decided I could come up with a better way to accomplish that."

He planted a brief kiss on her lips. "I think I'd better save the rest for dessert."

* * *

The following morning, Amanda awakened to find herself alone in bed. She vaguely remembered Drew leaving the bed sometime earlier. She donned her robe that lay at the foot of the bed and made her way to the bathroom. A few minutes later, still dressed in her robe, she was on her way down the stairs.

Drew turned away from his task at the stove when she entered the kitchen. He, too, was clad only in a robe. "Good morning, sleepyhead."

Amanda helped herself to coffee. "For your information, I considered trying to go back to sleep, but my stomach wouldn't let me. What's for breakfast?"

Drew looked up at the clock on the wall. "I think brunch might be a more appropriate term."

His sentence was punctuated by Amanda's stomach growling.

"You're really starving, aren't you? Must be a result of all that exercise last night."

Amanda ignored his remark.

Drew smiled. "In answer to your question, we're having French toast and sausage."

A few minutes later they sat down to breakfast. "What time should we leave for Nicole and David's place?"

"Maybe around one-thirty. I'm sure the two of you want time to visit before dinner."

After breakfast, Drew suggested she leave the cleanup to him. She went back upstairs and, after making the bed, decided she had plenty of time for a bubble bath.

She had been immersed in the bubbles for about fifteen minutes when the door opened and Drew entered with a grin on his face. He untied the belt of his robe and it fell open. Amanda's hand, holding the sponge, stopped in midair. Her gaze was fixed on the body with which she had become intimately acquainted in the past weeks. The temperature of the water seemed to suddenly increase ten degrees.

"Need any help?" he murmured, sauntering over to the tub and kneeling beside it. She focused her attention on his face and the desire burning in his eyes.

When she failed to respond to his question, Drew took the sponge from her hand. Her gaze never left his as he began gently smoothing it over her body. After completing his ministrations, he stood up and lifted her out of the tub. He toweled her off and began applying the lotion. When he knelt to smooth the lotion on her legs, she clutched his shoulders to keep from collapsing in a heap.

Moments later, they were lying in bed and his lips continued where his hands had left off. Amanda was involved in her own explorations. Her fingers caressed the flexing muscles of his arms and shoulders. When he finally entered her, she moaned.

"I think if I make love to you morning, noon, and night for the next fifty years, it still won't be enough."

They clung to each other, the ever-increasing rhythm bringing them closer to ecstasy. Seconds after she cried out his name, her body's spasms of pleasure sent him over the edge. He collapsed on top of her, then immediately shifted his body.

She clung to him, unwilling to let go. It felt so good holding him close to her.

"Don't leave me."

He kissed her tenderly. "Never, I promise, but I'm too heavy," he insisted.

"It feels good."

His smile was one of total satisfaction. He rolled over onto his back, taking her with him, their bodies still joined. He would have been content to stay in that position for hours. His hands caressed her body in long, smooth strokes.

After a while he sighed, breaking the spell. "I suppose Nicole would never speak to us again if we didn't show up for dinner."

Amanda lifted her chin from his chest and looked into his eyes. "I think she'd forgive us, eventually. The problem would be coming up with an excuse."

"You mean we can't tell her the truth?"

Amanda pinched him playfully and, with some difficulty, detached herself from him. Drew reluctantly let her go, grinning in admiration as she padded across the carpet to the bathroom.

It was after two o'clock when they pulled into the driveway of Nicole and David's house. Nicole smiled when she opened the door. She had been thrilled when Amanda told her about their plan to reconcile. She had always believed that they loved each other. She had even said a few prayers over the years that they would resolve their differences and get back together. Seeing them now, she knew she had been right about their feelings for each other.

"I'm glad you decided to join us," she said, taking their coats. "Everyone else is here already. Dinner will be ready soon."

"Is there anything I can do to help?" Amanda offered.

"No, thanks. Everything's under control. Mom *and* Erica insisted on bringing desserts; just one dessert for Thanksgiving dinner would never do."

The afternoon passed pleasantly. In addition to Nicole's parents and sister, Erica, the group included Erica's husband and infant daughter. The men were engrossed in football, but managed to pull themselves from the television long enough to eat dinner. They even half-heartedly offered to help clean up.

As the two of them cleared the table, Erica commented on the fact that she and Drew had arrived together. "Nicole told me the news. I'm so happy for you. After seeing the two of you together at Nicole's wedding, I wasn't really surprised."

"It seems that no one was surprised by my so-called news."

Erica laughed. "If you wanted it to be a surprise, you shouldn't have let anyone see you together. When you two look at each other, your feelings are obvious. I hope that doesn't embarrass you. I think it's great."

Amanda thought about the hour she and Drew had spent together just prior to leaving the house. She remembered hearing or reading that there was a certain look a woman exhibited after making love. She hoped it was just one of those things people say, but that has no foundation in truth.

"Thanks, Erica. No, that doesn't embarrass me." *If you could read my mind,* she thought, *it would be an entirely different matter, though.*

Friday was spent relaxing. Amanda used part of the time writing her resume and making a list of possible employers. Drew had insisted there was no hurry for her to find a job, but she knew she would never be content to sit around the house. If nothing else materialized, there was always the possibility of volunteer work. She was sure that plenty of agencies would be happy to accept any help offered free of charge.

The rest of the weekend was full. Saturday, they shopped for dining room furniture. They had decided that any other changes or additions to the house could wait. And there was still Amanda's furniture to be considered. Her bedroom furniture would fill one of the empty bedrooms, but the placement of the other pieces was still undecided.

Sunday, they went to the church Amanda had attended before moving away. The minister was the same one who had been there during her childhood. She had spoken with him the previous week and he had agreed to perform the ceremony to renew their vows. After the service, the two of them met with Rev. Walters and set the date for the last week of January.

Later that afternoon, Amanda prepared to leave. Drew watched as she packed the few items she had brought with her. When they had decided to reconcile, he convinced her to leave a supply of toiletries and even a few clothes at his house. She had just closed her bag when Drew came up behind her. Wrapping his arms around her, he nuzzled her neck.

"At the risk of sounding like a male chauvinist, I have to tell you that I was tempted to come and get you and drive you home this weekend. I worry about you."

Amanda turned in his arms and stretched up to plant a chaste kiss on his lips. "Drew, I appreciate your concern, but I promise to be careful. It's only an hour's drive and I'll be home before dark."

He nodded. "I know, I know."

After seeing her to her car, he kissed her again. "Call me when you get home," he instructed.

The next few weeks passed quickly. On one hand, Amanda was glad. It brought her closer to the time when she and Drew would be together. On the other hand, it brought her closer to Christmas and she was not looking forward to spending that day with Drew's family, or more precisely, his mother.

She had shopped and shopped, but could come up with no acceptable gift for her mother-in-law. She finally gave up. When Drew visited a week before the holiday, she explained her dilemma. They were in the process of decorating the small tree Amanda had insisted on buying.

"Amanda, I wish you had told me sooner. There was no need for you to put yourself through that. I've already bought them a gift, from both of us."

She shrugged. "I didn't think about that. I assumed the proper thing to do was buy them a gift myself. I'm glad that's settled."

"Speaking of Christmas gifts, what would you like?"

"Drew, you've already given me enough. I don't need anything else."

"Nothing?"

"Nothing." She raised her eyebrow. "Drew, you didn't buy me a gift, did you?"

"Just a little something." He grinned at his choice of words.

"I'm not sure what that grin means, but you look like the cat that ate the canary."

Drew laughed. "You'll find out what it means on Christmas morning."

The evening before Christmas Eve, Drew came to pick her up. She had tried to talk him out of it, to no avail. On the way back to Philadelphia, they stopped for dinner.

"Is there anything special that you want to do tomorrow?"

"Not really," she replied. An idea struck her immediately and she corrected her statement. "That's not true. Do they still have the candlelight service at church?"

"Yes, but I have to confess I haven't attended in the past few years."

"I'd like to go. I've missed that. None of the churches I've been attending have had that. I used to enjoy it a lot."

Drew nodded in agreement. "You know, you're right. I used to enjoy it, too. I just got out the habit of going. It sounds like a good idea."

The Christmas Eve service was just as Amanda remembered. The church was decorated with dozens of poinsettias and pillar candles. Each person was given a small candle that was lit near the end of the service, and the church became alive with flickering lights as the congregation sang "Silent Night."

Amanda looked up at the sky as they walked to the car. "You know what would make this perfect?"

Drew chuckled. "As far as you're concerned, I can guess. Snow?"

"It's been a long time since we had a white Christmas in this area. Admit it—you enjoy it, too."

"To tell you the truth, it's never been a big deal for me. Of course, under the present circumstances, I could change my mind."

"The present circumstances?"

At that moment, they reached the car. After he unlocked the door, he took her in his arms and kissed her.

"The circumstances of having you here with me. I have a vision in my mind of us being snowbound for a week with a roaring fire in the fireplace. The possibilities are endless."

Amanda grinned. "You mean like popping popcorn and roasting marshmallows?"

Drew laughed. "That's not exactly what I had in mind. In fact, I was looking at all those clothes you unpacked yesterday. Snow or no snow, I don't plan for you to need any of them, except when we go out for dinner tomorrow."

Eight

On Christmas morning, Amanda opened her eyes and stretched languorously. It took her a moment to realize she was alone in bed. Throwing back the covers, she retrieved her robe from the foot of the bed. She had just exited the bathroom when Drew entered the bedroom carrying a tray.

"Good morning and Merry Christmas."

"Merry Christmas. What's all this?"

"I had planned to surprise you with breakfast in bed. I didn't expect you to be awake yet."

He carried the tray to the small round table in the sitting area at the far end of the bedroom. Amanda followed him. He set the tray down and took her in his arms. Amanda twined her arms around his neck.

"You're going to spoil me, Drew."

"Good, that's exactly what I had in mind."

When he kissed her, she leaned into him. His arms tightened around her for a brief moment before he reluctantly broke the kiss.

"I think we'd better sit down to breakfast. I could get distracted very easily."

"There's something I have to get from downstairs, first. I had no idea we'd be eating breakfast up here."

She returned a few minutes later with a large square package. She handed it to Drew.

"I think I'll wait to open it."

After breakfast, Drew pulled a small box from the pocket of his robe. Handing it to Amanda, he reminded her, "I told you it was just a little something."

"Open yours first," she insisted.

Drew unwrapped the package and lifted the top off the box. Pushing aside the tissue paper, he found a small rectangular box. Inside the box was a gold chain-link identity bracelet.

"It's beautiful, Amanda."

"Somehow, a sweater just didn't seem enough. There's an inscription."

Drew turned the bracelet over and read, "To Drew, for being there for me, for having faith in me and, most of all, for loving me. All my love, Amanda."

"I don't know what to say, except that loving you is the easiest thing I've ever done."

He pointed to the unopened box on the table. "Your turn."

Amanda opened the small box expecting to find earrings or a pin. Instead, she found a ring, a beautiful, perfect, square-cut diamond.

"I decided it was time you had an engagement ring. There's a matching band, but I wanted to wait until the ceremony to put it on your finger when we say those vows. Is that alright?"

Tears sprang to her eyes. "It's beautiful, Drew, and I like your suggestion about the wedding band."

She rose from her chair and went to sit on his lap. "You are the kindest, most wonderful person I've ever known. How did I ever get so lucky?"

"Baby, that makes two of us. I love you, Amanda, more than anything."

* * *

Later that afternoon, Amanda prepared for dinner with Drew's parents. Getting dressed was just a small part of her preparation. The mental preparation required much more effort. She promised herself that she would not allow Drew's mother to upset her.

She had chosen a hunter green wool knit A-line dress with a round neck and long, fitted sleeves. Matching pumps and a gold chain and earrings completed the outfit. She stood in front of the mirror and sighed. Drew came from across the room and took her in his arms.

"You look beautiful, Amanda. Stop worrying."

She shrugged. "I'm not worried, just a little nervous."

He hugged her and kissed her forehead. "You'll be fine."

When they arrived at the Connors' home, Jennifer greeted Amanda with a hug. It appeared they were the last to arrive. Drew introduced her to the group assembled in the living room, which consisted of a few of the Connors' neighbors and Jennifer's fiancé, Morgan.

Drew's father was cordial, if not overly friendly, but his mother barely acknowledged her. In spite of that, Amanda was determined to enjoy herself. Her resolve was a little shaken when the last of the guests arrived. She would have been even angrier, had she noticed Claire's reaction.

Claire smiled triumphantly when her daughter went to answer door. She was certain of the identity of the caller. All other guests were already present.

Claire had encountered Deidre on a shopping trip a week earlier. When she had inquired after Deidre's parents, the young woman informed her that they were spending Christmas with her brother and his family.

Claire seized upon the opportunity, lamenting that it was a shame Deidre would be spending the holiday alone. Deidre assured her she was accustomed to it and did not mind, since she would be on duty at the hospital until early afternoon. Claire insisted she join them; she would be off duty in plenty of time for dinner. Deidre finally acquiesced.

When Jennifer returned from answering the door, she was accompanied by a beautiful young woman whom Amanda had never seen before. Jennifer opened her mouth to introduce her, but Drew's mother forestalled her.

"Deidre, I'm so glad you could join us," Claire gushed, hugging her. "I imagine it wasn't easy with your busy schedule. Everyone, I'd like you to meet Dr. Deidre Thornton."

For the rest of the afternoon, Amanda's patience was put to the test. Claire raved about Deidre continuously. Amanda learned that Deidre and Drew had dated steadily in high school, but grew apart when they went off to different colleges. Deidre was still single and it appeared that Claire was determined to remedy that situation, with her son. The fact that Drew was not single was no deterrent, as far as Claire was concerned.

Aside from trying to cope with his mother's attitude, she was upset that Drew appeared oblivious to the subtle but deliberate spitefulness that never abated. Deep down, she knew that was unfair. She was the one who had assured Drew that she could handle his mother's animosity. She had also promised herself that she would not be responsible for driving a wedge between Drew and his family.

Keeping that promise in mind, Amanda was determined not to let Claire's machinations ruin the day. She kept reminding herself that it was Christmas, the season of peace and good will. She would not put Drew in the middle of a power struggle between herself and his mother.

She felt better about the situation as she observed Drew and Deidre more closely. They were friendly, but she had to admit there was no hint of anything more than two friends reminiscing over old times.

That particular observation pleased Amanda, but it was very disappointing for Claire. If the fact that Drew and Deidre seemed to have no romantic interest in each other was not enough to ruin her day, Amanda seemed totally unconcerned over the presence of Drew's former girlfriend. She had actually seen her talking to Deidre and smiling.

Amanda was glad when Drew suggested it was time to leave. Contrary to appearances, she was exhausted from her efforts to maintain a pleasant facade. Keeping the peace with Claire was not an easy task.

Later that night, Claire sat at her dressing table, removing her makeup. She thought back over the events of the day. She was disappointed with the meeting between Drew and Deidre.

She would never admit it, but her actions had been prompted more by an effort to make Amanda uncomfortable than any hope that Drew and Deidre would be drawn to each other. After all, it had been almost fifteen years since they had dated.

The underlying truth was that she had distrusted Drew's wife years earlier. She had clung to that opinion and the belief that her son deserved better.

Kenneth's statement interrupted her musings. "It didn't work, Claire."

Claire spun around to face him. "What do you mean?"

Kenneth gazed directly at her. He did not respond immediately.

Claire became uncomfortable under his scrutiny. She was on the brink of turning away, or repeating her question. She was still trying to decide which to do when he spoke.

"I think you know what I mean. Before you invited her to dinner, when was the last time you saw, or even spoke to, Deidre Thornton?"

"What difference does that make? I ran into her when I was shopping. She was planning to spend the holidays alone. I was only being courteous when I invited her to dinner."

"Claire, I'm not going to belabor the point. It's not necessary to make excuses to me. I'm simply voicing my observations. What I do hope is that you think about your real motives and, at least, be honest with yourself."

Claire said nothing. She turned back to the mirror and continued with her nightly ritual. She tried to ignore her husband's remarks. They had hit their mark and she had already admitted as much to herself. But she was not willing to openly concede that fact to him.

It was still early evening when Amanda and Drew reached home. Drew helped her off with her coat. "That wasn't so bad, was it? I thought the afternoon went rather well."

Amanda bit back the words that were on the tip of her tongue. How could he not see Deidre's presence for what it was? Amanda had heard his mother's explanation for including Deidre in the festivities. Did he really think her only motivation was concern that a close friend not spend the holiday alone?

She tried to see the situation from his point of view. She supposed she would feel compelled to give her the benefit of the doubt if it was her mother.

As hard as it was, she would bide her time. Either Claire would slip up and show her true colors in front of Drew, or she would finally give up and accept their marriage.

When he turned to hang their coats in the closet, Amanda headed for the kitchen.

"I feel like a cup of tea. What about you? Shall I make some coffee?"

"That sounds good."

A short time later, he carried the tray with their mugs into the living room. Amanda kicked off her shoes and, lifting her mug, settled back on the over-stuffed sofa. Aside from the Christmas tree lights, the only other light in the room was the subdued glow of a lamp in the corner.

Drew took a sip of coffee and rose from his seat to retrieve a flat box from beneath the tree. Returning to the sofa, he handed her the box.

"The ring wasn't the only 'little something' I bought for you."

As she unwrapped it, he added, cryptically, "I'm not sure if that's for you, or for me."

Pushing aside the tissue paper, Amanda revealed a vision of black lace. She had no need to lift it out of the box to know it was a nightie, the likes of which she doubted she would have purchased for herself.

"You actually went into a store and bought this?" she asked, eyebrows raised.

Drew chuckled. "I've passed the shop for weeks, looking at it and envisioning you in it. I knew I'd never be satisfied until I made that vision a reality."

He moved closer and took her in his arms. After a long, searing kiss, he murmured against her lips, "I think now it's time for my part of this gift."

Breathlessly, Amanda repeated, "Your part of the gift?"

He nodded and released her. "Try it on."

She stood up and started toward the doorway, expecting him to follow her. He had settled back against the sofa.

"Aren't you coming? I thought you'd want to make sure it fits."

"Why don't you come back here and model it for me?"

A short time later she returned, clad in her robe. Drew frowned.

"Don't tell me it didn't fit?"

Amanda opened the robe and let it drop to the floor. After twirling around, she faced him and asked, "What do you think?"

Drew's gaze was glued to the vision before him. He rose from his seat and walked slowly toward her. She could barely hear his words when he finally spoke.

"What do I think? I think, 'Merry Christmas to me.' "

Lifting her into his arms, he walked across the hall and up the stairs. Her arms entwined around his neck, Amanda began sprinkling kisses along his cheek. Not content with that, she nibbled his ear, while her fingers massaged the nape of his neck.

"If you keep that up, lady, we may not make it to the bedroom. It might be interesting to find out if it's possible to make love on the stairs."

Amanda squeezed his neck and laughed softly. "I know you're very inventive, but I think that might be beyond even your abilities."

"Is that a challenge?"

Amanda immediately backed down. "No way. I'm not in the mood to go tumbling down the stairs, thank you."

They reached the bedroom and Drew noticed she had already turned down the covers. Before long, her newest Christmas gift was lying on the chair on top of the clothes he had shed in record time. Sometime later, they were asleep in each other's arms.

The day after Christmas, they returned to Amanda's apartment for a few days. She would be moving in with Drew two days before the ceremony to renew their vows near the end of January. She had explained to him that she needed to use part of her week's vacation to pack, and he insisted on helping.

David and Nicole had promised to help with the actual move, and Amanda had already reserved a truck. Most of the dishes and small appliances would be donated to charity, but that was only a very small part of her possessions.

They worked steadily for two days, packing and stacking boxes. The nights were spent engaged in more pleasant activities. Amanda was amazed at the passion that seemed insatiable. Even after making love the night before, she often had to force her gaze from him and attend to her own tasks. More than once she was tempted to suggest a break from their routine, but not for the purpose of resting.

They returned to Philadelphia the day before New Year's Eve with most of Amanda's clothes and books. She had left just enough clothes in her apartment to see her through the next few weeks.

As she hung her clothes in one of the large walk-in

closets in the bedroom, Amanda was startled to feel tears welling up in her eyes. She exited the closet and almost ran into Drew, coming to see if she had sufficient hangers for her clothes.

"Amanda? You're crying. What's wrong?"

He held his breath. He was wary of asking the question that immediately came to his mind, but he had to know the truth. He lifted her chin so she was forced to meet his gaze.

"Are you having second thoughts, Amanda?"

Amanda was startled by the apprehension she saw in his eyes. She reached up and caressed his cheek, shaking her head.

"Oh, Drew, no, not at all. In fact, I was just thinking I can't believe that soon I'll be back here for good. I've never been more sure of anything than I am about this move."

She pulled his head down to hers, punctuating her statement with a warm, sweet kiss. "I love you, Drew."

He embraced her, but she gently pulled away, smiling. "Right now, however, we'd better finish getting those boxes and the rest of my clothes out of the car."

The Sunday after New Year's Day, Drew reluctantly drove Amanda back to her apartment. He was tempted to stay overnight, but he had an early appointment the following morning. He stayed only a few minutes after seeing her safely inside.

Amanda's workload eased off in the next two weeks. All of her patients at the center had been assigned to other counselors, and the schools had hired replacements. By the second week in January, she had completed her reports and more of her packing.

She suggested to Sharon that she would like to give a party to say good-bye to her young patients. She would miss them. The party was as much for her as it was to show them she thought they were special. They had decided to include all of the children, not just Amanda's patients.

The children had been told she was leaving to get married. Typical for their ages, the girls were excited and asked a number of questions, most of which Amanda deftly sidestepped.

She had never expected them to bring gifts for her. In fact, she thought she had made it clear that the party was for them. Most of their families had little money, but their initiative and creativity touched her.

When she opened the gift from Maya, tears came to her eyes. She had observed that the child had a special gift for drawing, but she never realized the extent of her talent until she unwrapped the beautiful watercolor scene.

"It's a lake near my grandma's house. Mom and I went there this summer."

Amanda nodded. "I remember when you told me you were going to visit your grandmother. You're very lucky to have such a beautiful place to visit."

She hugged the child. "And I'm very lucky to have a picture of such a beautiful place. You have a real talent, Maya. Don't ever stop using it."

Her last day of work at the center was just a few days before she was scheduled to move. She was surprised to find only the receptionist present when she arrived.

"Where is everyone?"

"I think Sharon's in the conference room." She handed her a folder. "Would you take this to her, please?"

"Sure."

Amanda had barely opened the door to the conference room when she was greeted by shouts. "Surprise!"

Sharon was the first to reach her as everyone crowded around to hug her and congratulate her. "You didn't think we'd let you go without a party, did you?"

"I thought the party last week was it."

"That was for the kids. We had to have a separate party for what we have planned."

Amanda was puzzled by those words until she began opening the gifts. Her coworkers had decided that it was unlikely she needed any household items. With that in mind, they had all given her lingerie. As she opened box after box of luxury bath items and filmy, lacy nighties, the latter brought back memories of Drew's Christmas present.

Amanda received another surprise when Drew arrived with the moving van a few days later. In addition to David and Nicole, he was accompanied by Jennifer and Morgan. Amanda was in the process of packing the last few items when the crew arrived.

Drew took charge of organizing the men and carrying the furniture and larger boxes to the truck. Nicole and Jennifer set to work helping Amanda pack the remainder of household items and books she was taking with her.

Midway through the day, they stopped to eat lunch. Amanda looked around at the group sitting on the floor eating sandwiches and realized what had been missing from her life for the past six years, and even longer than that. While she was friendly with her coworkers, she had never really made any other close friends since Nicole.

Her social life had been very limited. By the time she was a teenager, her father had become so belligerent that she never had friends over to visit. She had a few dates, but his questions and accusations had soon put and end to them. The boys decided she was not worth the inquisitions, and she decided it was not worth the verbal abuse.

Since leaving Philadelphia, she had been busy—first with school, and later with her work. She had never known the enjoyment of an informal gathering with a few friends.

Nine

Drew watched Amanda out of the corner of his eye as she prepared for the ceremony. Clad only in ivory lace underwear and thigh-high stockings, she sat at the dressing table applying her makeup. She had his full attention when she rose and walked to her closet. She returned a few minutes later wearing an ivory wool crepe A-line dress with a low-cut neckline and thin straps. She walked over to him.

"Would you zip me up, please?" she asked, turning her back to him.

Drew finished buttoning his shirt and turned toward her. After placing the fingers of one hand on the zipper just below the small of her back, he paused.

"Do I have to?" he murmured, the fingers of his other hand tracing a path up her spine.

Amanda shivered slightly and reached behind her in an attempt to still the hand that was wreaking havoc with her senses. "We don't have time for this, Drew."

He heaved an exaggerated sigh. "Oh well, if you insist."

He zipped the dress but before she could move away, he clutched her shoulders. Leaning over, he placed a kiss at the nape of her neck.

Amanda took a deep breath and, with some effort, pulled away from him and returned to her closet.

She donned the matching pearl- and lace-trimmed jacket and ivory pumps. A moment later, she rejoined him in the bedroom.

Amanda stood arm in arm with Drew in front of Reverend Walters in the almost empty sanctuary of the church she had attended since childhood. The same group that had helped her move were present to witness the event. Besides the young people, the group included Nicole's parents and, surprisingly, Drew's father, Kenneth.

When Amanda had uttered the solemn vows eight years earlier, she had been in somewhat of a daze. This time, she listened to each word and repeated her vows with a renewed and more complete sense of commitment. This time it felt right; there were none of the doubts and fears that had plagued her before.

She looked into Drew's eyes as he repeated his vows and she saw the same promise of love and devotion that was reflected in her own. After placing the simple band on her finger, he turned her hand over and kissed her palm.

Just before planting a brief kiss on her lips he murmured, "This time it's forever."

Following the ceremony, Amanda received her second surprise of the day. She had expected that she and Drew would share a quiet dinner afterward. Instead, Kenneth had arranged a celebratory dinner for the group at a fancy restaurant.

Claire was conspicuous in her absence. No one mentioned her or questioned her reason for not attending the ceremony. Her animosity toward Amanda was well-known.

Amanda sympathized with Kenneth. He seemed to

be enjoying himself, but she could not help thinking that it had to be a very difficult position for him.

Her father's absence had also been expected. At first, she had no intention of telling him she had returned to Philadelphia, let alone invite him to the ceremony. It was only at Drew's urging that she relented. She did not ask him if he planned to attend. She simply called and told him the date and time, making him aware of this change in her life.

She knew that Nicole's mother had informed her father of her leaving more than six years ago, and Nicole had told her about the disagreement she and her mother had had over that.

Nicole's mother had insisted that he had a right to know his daughter had left the area. What neither of them told Amanda was that his response restrained Charlotte from offering any further information concerning his daughter's whereabouts.

Amanda never asked about his reaction. She correctly assumed that as far as he was concerned, it had to be something she had done wrong.

In spite of the absent relatives, the party was a festive affair. They had a room at the restaurant to themselves, but as the evening progressed, the music from the next room filtered in.

Nicole nudged David. "See, we don't need our own DJ."

She looked around the room. "We have plenty of space; we might as well take advantage of the situation."

As Nicole and David made their way to the open area, Drew took Amanda's hand and stood up. The music next door was a slow, romantic ballad and Amanda's heartbeat accelerated as his arms came around her. She was amazed that such a simple gesture could have this effect, but she had no doubt it would always be so.

The snow started falling just as they exited the restaurant. When they reached home, there was already a solid coating of snow on the driveway. Drew grinned as he opened the car door for her.

"That's what I call perfect timing."

He closed the door behind her and turned to see her frowning. "What do you mean?"

"You mean you've forgotten my plans for being snowbound? I guess it's too much to hope this will continue and shut down the city for weeks, but I guess I'll just have to make the most of it."

They walked up the stairs arm in arm. When they reached the bedroom, he took her in his arms, but she pulled back.

"Why don't you build the fire you've been wanting, while I take a bubble bath and slip into something more comfortable."

"Hmm, I like the sound of that."

Half an hour later, Amanda emerged from the bathroom dressed in her velour robe. Drew closed the fireplace screen, then stood up and turned to face her. He raised an eyebrow as he looked her up and down. Amanda smiled at the disappointment written all over his face. She walked over to him and began unbuttoning his shirt.

"I had to be sure the fire had taken the chill out of the room."

He untied the belt of her robe and it fell open, revealing a sheer slip of a gown in teal green. Although it was floor-length, it hid nothing. Drew stilled her hands long enough to ease the robe from her shoulders and push it to the floor.

Amanda continued with her task, but he was making it very difficult. His fingertips traced a feather-light path down the side of her neck, along her shoulder, back across her collarbone and down her breasts.

She took a deep breath when his hand dipped beneath the fabric to cup one enticing globe. She managed to finish her task and he shrugged out of his shirt. She inhaled the enticing scent that surrounded him while her hands splayed across his chest.

Drew nibbled her ear, murmuring, "Do you really think you'll need that fire in the fireplace to take the chill off? I'm sure I can manage that better than a few flaming logs."

Within minutes, she had disposed of the last of his clothes. He stood before her, totally unself-conscious in his nakedness. He eased her down on the pillows in front of the fireplace. His hands continued their magic, his fingers probing and caressing until she thought she would explode from the sheer pleasure.

When she moaned his name, Drew quickly stripped off the filmy garment. He gazed at her for a long moment, she was so beautiful. Her own scent, mingled with her perfume, surrounded him as he eased his body between her thighs. He kissed her with all the love and desire that had been building in him since he had uttered his promise to love and cherish.

"Sweetheart, you're a feast for the senses. Every time I look at you, I want to touch this soft, silky skin."

His tongue traced the same pattern his fingers had drawn earlier. "You taste so good."

Amanda moaned when his lips continued their path down her body. "I love those little sounds you make," he whispered, his lips fueling the fire inside her.

When he entered her, her body welcomed him. They moved together as if they had been made for each other. Moments later, she cried out his name. Her body contracted in the aftermath of ecstasy, sending him over the edge. He laid there for a while, feeling the rhythm of her heartbeat in time with his own.

When he rolled over on his side, he saw that she was almost asleep. She murmured when he lifted her in his arms and carried her to the bed. After banking the fire, he returned to the bed. She was slumbering peacefully and, within minutes he, too, was sound asleep with her in his arms.

The next morning, Amanda awakened alone in bed. She only vaguely remembered Drew carrying her to bed, although she recalled every detail of their love-making. She stretched slowly and was on the verge of getting out of bed when Drew entered carrying a large tray. After depositing it on the bench at the foot of the bed, he came around to the side of the bed, leaned over and kissed her.

"Good morning."

Amanda sat up, placing her hands on his shoulders. "Breakfast in bed? I warned you before, I'm going to get spoiled and you won't have anyone to blame but yourself."

She gestured to the alcove. "I just have one question. Are you actually going to serve me in bed or should we eat at the table over there?"

"Now that you mention it, I think the coffee might be safer at the table."

"In that case, would you hand me my robe, please?"

"No."

Amanda was surprised at his refusal until he grinned. "I'm not going to hand you your robe. As a matter of fact, I'm going to stand right here and enjoy watching you walk across the room. I think that pleasure is small payment for slaving over a hot stove all morning."

Amanda remembered all the days and nights of lovemaking. She refused to be embarrassed at this late date. Throwing back the covers, she rose and strolled across the room. Instead of picking up her robe, she took a seat at the table and folded her hands. Not to be outdone, Drew shed his robe, picked up the tray and joined her.

Amanda lifted the lids from the plates as he poured the coffee. She helped herself to French toast and bacon, trying to ignore him. Her mind's image of what was hidden beneath the table was even more intoxicating than the bare chest directly in her line of vision.

Drew filled his own plate but he could barely keep his eyes on his food. He took a deep breath when she began pouring syrup on her French toast.

They managed to get through the meal in spite of the distractions, although there was little conversation. Amanda poured a second cup of coffee for each of them while he began stacking their empty dishes.

"I had an interesting thought when you were pouring the syrup on your French toast."

If she had not answered so quickly, she might have guessed what was on his mind. "What?"

"I was waiting for you to accidentally trickle a little of it down between those beautiful breasts. Being the gentleman that I am, I would have offered to clean it off for you."

Amanda slowly stirred her coffee. She looked over at the fireplace to assure herself that the logs had not spontaneously burst into flames. A brief glance told her that the only fire was inside her body. She looked up and met his gaze, and knew that it wasn't just her body.

Of one accord they rose from their chairs. Their bodies met, heated skin to heated skin. There was no friction, but the mere contact of their nude flesh had the same effect as that of rubbing two sticks together. The passion that had been simmering since they had sat down to breakfast erupted instantly.

Ten

The following week, Amanda had her first taste of what she had always dreamed married life would be. Drew had left her in charge of completing the task of decorating their home. After the dining room furniture was delivered on Tuesday, Amanda began shopping for accessories. Her bedroom furniture had been set up in one of the extra bedrooms, and she was in the process of turning it into a guest room. Her bookcases and other furniture had been temporarily placed in another of the extra bedrooms.

In addition to the shopping, Amanda had squeezed in four job interviews. Two looked promising, but she might not know anything for weeks. Meanwhile, she was enjoying a hiatus from her previous hectic existence.

When she had left Drew, she had already completed one year of college. Between a small educational loan and the money in the bank, she had had enough money to pay another year's college tuition, as well as living expenses for a few months. She found a job and for three years, she worked full-time and attended school full-time. Her social life had been nonexistent.

Her first respite had come in the few months between graduation and the start of her first real position as a counselor. In addition to her counseling duties, she continued school. She had obtained her master's degree less than a year before Drew came back into her life.

Although she and Drew had their separate responsibilities during the day, the evenings were reserved for their own special time together. Amanda had always enjoyed cooking, but she had never had the time to indulge that particular pleasure.

After dinner, they sometimes adjourned to the library to watch a movie. More often, they settled in the sitting area of the bedroom where Drew would build a fire and they would simply listen to music and talk. Whichever room they chose, the evening inevitably ended in making love, sometimes slowly and thoroughly, and sometimes in an instant explosion of passion.

Amanda's newfound wedded bliss lasted barely a week after the ceremony. They had just finished dinner one night when their evening was interrupted by a telephone call from Jennifer.

"Hi, Drew. How's everything going, as if I need to ask. I haven't heard from either of you since the ceremony."

"We've been busy."

Jennifer laughed. "I'll just bet you have."

"Alright, Jen, have your fun now. You have a wedding coming up soon, and a honeymoon."

"Okay, big brother. That's not what I called for, anyway. Has Dad talked to you this week?"

"No. Why? Is anything wrong?"

"No. I guess he'll get around to calling you. He's been planning a big birthday bash for Mom."

"When?"

"The fourth of next month. I just wanted to give you a heads-up before he calls you. I know the idea of attending another celebration in Mom's company isn't going to go over big with Amanda."

"You're right. Hopefully, Mom's learned since Christmas that it's time to accept our relationship."

When Drew hung up the telephone, Amanda turned from her task of putting the dishes in the dishwasher. She could not help overhearing Drew's part of the conversation and she had no qualms about questioning him.

"What was that all about?"

"Jennifer says Dad's planning a big birthday party for Mom in a couple of weeks."

Amanda went back to her task. "That's nice."

Drew walked over to her. Her back was to him and as his arms encircled her, he asked, "What does that mean?"

She shrugged. "Just that. I imagine it's always nice to have a special celebration for your birthday."

She wriggled out of his embrace and walked over to the table. "I'm sure you and Jennifer will enjoy it, too."

"What about you?"

"I'm not going, Drew."

"You have to go." He knew it was the wrong thing to say as soon as the words left his mouth.

Her hand stopped in midair as she reached for a bowl on the table. She turned to face him.

"Excuse me."

Drew held up his hands "Alright, I take that back. Amanda, I would like for you to accompany me."

"I'm sorry, Drew, but your politeness isn't going to change my mind. I'm not going to your mother's birthday party."

"Well, if that's your final decision, fine. I won't go either."

"You have to go."

Drew raised an eyebrow. "Excuse me."

She shook her head. "You know what I mean. It's not the same. She's your mother. You should be there for her."

"Maybe, but you should be there, too, for me."

"You don't need me there, Drew. You're just being stubborn."

They debated the issue for a few more minutes, neither willing to back down. The debate was very close to becoming an argument when Amanda ended the discussion."

"You do whatever you like. Whether you attend the party is *your* decision. Whether I attend is *my* decision and I will not be going to the party."

After delivering that final statement, she left the room before he could respond. Drew stood staring for a few minutes. He had never expected her to be so adamant in her decision. The longer he thought about it, the more upset he became with himself. He, more than anyone else, should be able to understand her refusal to come into contact with his mother any more than necessary.

If he had asked her at that moment, Amanda could not have explained exactly why she was so determined not to go to the party. She had survived the Christmas dinner and had not had any contact with Claire since that day. Maybe the woman was coming around.

After she thought about it for a few minutes, Amanda realized that one problem was her belief that Drew either did not recognize the extent of Claire's malice, or chose to overlook it as being unimportant. That was reason enough for her refusal.

The other reason was that her life seemed so perfect now and she did not want to spoil it. She preferred to ignore the older woman's existence. She knew she was being illogical. She would have to come in contact with Claire again, eventually.

Amanda was angry with herself for letting their discussion get out of hand. She thought maybe a nice, hot bath would make her feel better, and as she lay there in the soothing bubbles it occurred to her that her aversion to Claire was not the only reason for her refusal to attend the party. There was another side to that decision.

When Amanda finished her bath and entered the bedroom, she was surprised to see Drew lounging on the loveseat. She had expected him to be angry at her parting words. She approached him slowly, gauging his mood.

Drew sighed. "You look as if you're afraid I might bite."

He motioned for her to sit down beside him. "At the risk of starting the argument again, I have to ask you to please think about coming to the party."

Amanda looked down at her hands. "Drew, do you remember before we got back together, what I told you when we discussed your mother's feelings toward me? I promised I wouldn't be responsible for coming between you and your family. That's what will happen if you refuse to go to the party."

"You can solve that problem by agreeing to come with me."

"It's not just my feelings that have to be considered. You know how your mother feels about me. I'm sure she would prefer not to have me there. Since it's her special celebration, I think she deserves to have her way."

He shook his head. "Not about this. She has to get used to the idea that a family celebration includes you. Besides, when you consider the number of guests that will be there, you'll probably only have minimal direct contact with her."

Amanda raised her head, looking him directly in the eye. "Drew, why is this so important to you?"

"Because you're my wife and you're part of the family. I don't think it's a good idea for you to stay away from a family gathering to appease my mother."

He put his arm around her, pulling her close. "There's another side to this, too."

She looked up at him. "What?"

"You don't like her, either."

She made no reply to that blunt but honest statement. He had a point, but she was not ready to concede.

"I'm not saying you don't have some legitimate reasons for your feelings. I'm just saying that avoiding her won't solve the problem. Will you think about it?"

"I'll think about it."

Two weeks later, Amanda stood in front of the bedroom mirror, assessing her image in preparation for Claire's birthday party. It meant so much to Drew that she had finally agreed to go.

He had insisted she buy a new dress for the occasion. She was so sensitive on the subject that at first, she thought he was hinting that none of her outfits were acceptable.

She was ashamed of that thought when he made it clear that his suggestion was prompted by the opinion that shopping for a new outfit would give her spirits a lift. It was clear to him that even though she had given in, she was not looking forward to the evening.

After hours of shopping, she had settled on a short, red velvet trapeze-style dress with long, fitted sleeves. The teardrop pearl earrings matched the pendant nestled close to her cleavage, revealed by the square neckline.

Drew entered from the bathroom as she turned from the mirror. His gaze traveled appreciatively from the neckline and its tempting decolletage to the hemline that stopped above her knees.

He cleared his throat. "I should have gone shopping with you. I'm not sure I like the idea of other men gaping at those beautiful legs."

Amanda grinned and sashayed over to him. Stretching up onto her toes, she planted a brief kiss on his mouth.

"Do you always know the right thing to say?"

Drew laughed and pulled her into his arms. "You, of all people, know better than that. I just manage to get it right every now and then."

His hand caressed the nape of her neck. "Besides, I'm only telling the truth." He kissed the tip of her nose. "I think we'd better get out of here or the party might be over by the time we arrive."

The festivities were in full swing when Drew and Amanda arrived at the restaurant. Amanda was relieved when she saw that Claire was engrossed with a group of her guests. Drew went to greet his parents. Amanda had no choice but to accompany him.

After a quick greeting, she made her escape. She was aware that it would be impolite not to offer her congratulations. She just wanted to put it off for a while.

Amanda managed to avoid Claire until the party was almost half over. She finally decided that good manners dictated she not delay any longer in wishing her a happy birthday. Drew was involved in conversation with Morgan. When he saw where Amanda was headed, he excused himself and followed her.

Amanda took a deep breath and approached Claire. "Hello, Mrs. Connors."

"Well, it's a little late in the evening for greetings, Amanda."

"I spoke to you earlier, but I guess you didn't hear me. There were several other guests around claiming your attention."

"I see." She looked her up and down. "I hadn't noticed it at Christmas, but you've gained weight over the years."

"Thank you," Amanda said. She forced herself to smile through clenched teeth.

Claire raised and eyebrow. "That wasn't a compliment."

It was Amanda's turn to raise an eyebrow. "That's strange. Drew seems to appreciate the extra pounds. Besides, I was sure it had to be a compliment. Otherwise, it would be a very rude remark."

"You're being impertinent."

"Not really, just honest," Amanda replied. "Before you say anything else, Mrs. Connors, I just came over to wish you a happy birthday. I hope you have many more, although I have my doubts about that. In fact, I wonder if you've ever had a happy birthday or any other day."

"You have no right to speak to me that way."

Amanda took her second deep breath since her decision to speak to her mother-in-law. "All things considered, Mrs. Connors, I think I have every right. I used to think there was something wrong with me that made you hate me. I've learned that the problem is not with me; it's with you. You're a very bitter woman. In spite of your feelings toward me, though, I do sincerely wish you a happy birthday."

Drew had heard the exchange and was amused by it until he saw the look on Amanda's face as she walked away without another word. Her eyes were strangely bright, as if there were tears glistening in them. Her control had exacted a price.

After a few words to his mother, he went looking for his wife, and he found her at the coat-check counter. The woman had just taken her coat from the rack and was preparing to hand it to her. Drew took her hand as she reached for the garment.

"What are you doing?"

"I'm leaving, Drew. You stay here and enjoy yourself. I'll call a taxi."

He took her other hand in his. "Do you really think I could enjoy myself?"

"I'm sorry. I probably shouldn't have said those things to your mother, but I couldn't hold it in any longer. I'm sorry if I ruined your evening."

Drew shook his head. He wiped away a tear that had escaped from the corner of her eye. He enfolded her in his arms.

"You've got it all wrong, sweetheart. You didn't ruin my evening with those words, but I can't enjoy myself if you leave."

"Drew, I can't stay here, now. Maybe I haven't ruined your evening, but I don't think you can say the same for your mother."

"Amanda, I heard the remark she made. I thought you showed considerable restraint in your response. I saw her face after you walked away and it didn't seem to me that she was terribly upset. If anyone's words upset her, it would be mine. I'm not even sure my words made any difference to her."

"What did you say to her?"

"I told her I wouldn't have been here if you hadn't agreed to come with me. I also told her that if she couldn't learn to be civil to you, she would see very little of me because I refuse to ask you to subject yourself to her insults."

"You really said that to her?" It was a question, but the expression on his face told her he was telling the truth.

"Yes, and I mean every word of it, Amanda. Unless she changes, the next time you tell me you don't want to come to an affair involving my mother, I won't try to talk you into it."

He looked at the woman behind the counter. "Would you put the coat back, please?"

The strains of a slow ballad wafted out into the hallway. Amanda looked up at him and he smiled. "It would be a shame to let that music go to waste, wouldn't it?"

The remainder of the evening passed pleasantly. Several times during the celebration, Amanda's gaze was drawn to her mother-in-law. In spite of her personal issues with Claire, she had not intended to ruin her celebration. It appeared that Drew was correct in his assessment. The older woman was enjoying the festivities and appeared to be unaffected by their earlier confrontation.

Eleven

The next morning, Claire found herself on the receiving end of another lecture. She had been feeling proud of herself in spite of the sharp words that had been spoken to her the previous evening. She was convinced that she would be vindicated in her attitude toward Amanda. She was pouring her third cup of coffee when her husband decided it was time for him to speak up.

"Claire, we need to talk."

His tone of voice earned her undivided attention. In their thirty-five years of marriage, she had never heard a harsh word from her husband. In fact, he usually let her have her way in everything. His curt words could only mean he was upset about some situation, maybe a problem with the business.

"What is it, Kenneth? Is everything alright? Are you ill?"

"No, Claire, I'm not ill. But everything is not alright."

He took a deep breath. He had not expected it would be easy to say the words he had to say, but he had let it go too long. It was obvious from her comments the previous evening that his hints concerning Amanda had had no effect on his wife. He had chosen not to go along with her attitude when he took part in Drew and Amanda's ceremony renewing their vows. He had made that choice, but had chosen not to inform his wife of that decision. It was time to be open and honest.

"I've kept silent for years, partly because I didn't approve of Drew's marriage, either. In my opinion, Amanda was too young and Drew was marrying her for the wrong reasons. That's no longer the case. They love each other, Claire. More importantly, they're good for each other."

Claire pursed her lips. Her entire body tensed as he spoke. "I see she has you fooled, too. I can't believe that neither of you can see that she's only after Drew's money and the material things he can give her. She's no different now than she was eight years ago."

"You may be right. If that's true, we both did her a great injustice eight years ago. Claire, she didn't pursue Drew eight years ago and she didn't pursue him a few months ago. He told us that himself, but you chose not to believe him."

He reached across the table and took her hand in his. "Claire, I know you don't want to face this, but you're in danger of losing your son. I heard what he said to you last night."

She jerked her hand away from his. "You heard the way he spoke to me and you didn't say anything!"

"There was nothing for me to say. He wasn't disrespectful. He expressed his feelings and he has that right. We raised our children with that freedom, remember?"

Kenneth shook his head. "Claire, if all you heard was his tone of voice, you missed the point. That's what I mean when I say that you're in danger of losing him.

"I went to the ceremony, the renewing of their vows. I watched the way they looked at each other and do you know what occurred to me?"

Claire looked around, fidgeting. Her disinterest in the entire conversation was obvious. Her discomfort with the discussion was even more evident, and that told him that he had to continue. He waited patiently for her response.

After some hesitation, she finally responded to his question. "What occurred to you, Kenneth?"

"It occurred to me that I can't ever recall your looking at me the way Amanda looked at our son. To tell you the truth, it made me feel a little jealous. It made me wonder if you ever loved me as much as Amanda loves our son."

"How can you say that! Just because I don't look at you a certain way doesn't mean I don't love you. You knew from the beginning that I'm not a very demonstrative person."

"You're right. I accepted that and it never stopped me from loving you."

He took her hand in his again. "I didn't mean to hurt you, Claire. You know I've never done anything to deliberately hurt you. I also know it's a two-way street. Maybe I haven't been as affectionate as I could be. Having realized my own shortcomings, I intend on my part to change.

"That doesn't solve the other problem, though. I've dropped a few hints for you before. After last night, I knew I had to tell you, straight out, that I think you're making a mistake with Drew and Amanda."

"I can't help it. I don't trust her."

"I know. I also know why you don't trust her. But she's not your mother, Claire. She's nothing like your mother."

Claire's eyes widened. "What do you know about my mother?"

"Honey, we've been married for thirty-five years. I know the whole story. I know how your grandparents would have nothing to do with your father because he married 'beneath him.' I know how your mother deserted you when he died and there was no financial help forthcoming from his parents. I know how she left you with the grandparents who reluctantly took you in.

"You've held on to that anger for a long time. When Amanda came along and Drew decided to marry her, all you could see was your mother taking advantage of your father and then leaving you alone. You refuse to see that the situation is entirely different and that Amanda's different. You've been taking that bitterness out on her and she's totally innocent."

"How long have you known all this? And who told you?"

"I've known since before we were married. One of your grandparents' neighbors told me. She had no idea she was revealing a secret. In fact, I think she was hinting that if she ever heard that I had mistreated you in any way, I'd have to answer to her. She said you'd already had more than your share of unhappiness."

"Mrs. Wilson," Claire murmured, a faraway look in her eyes. She remembered the woman just a few houses down the street who had always seemed to be smiling. "I'd almost forgotten how kind she was to me."

Kenneth wanted to say more, but he knew he had already given her enough to handle. She had to have time to digest the fact that he knew her secret. Even more important, she had to come to grips with the fact that he had voiced his disagreement with an attitude that had become ingrained in her.

He rose from his seat, walked over to her and pulled her out of her chair. Taking her in his arms, he kissed her gently but thoroughly.

"I love you, Claire. I'll always love you, no matter what, but I hope you'll think about what I've said. Drew and Amanda deserve a chance to live their lives without unnecessary problems from either of us."

   While Claire and Kenneth were having their discussion, Amanda and Drew were sharing a much more pleasant morning. Drew awakened alone in bed to the smell of coffee and bacon.

   Fifteen minutes later, he entered the kitchen. Leaning against the doorjamb, he watched Amanda take a pan out of the oven. He waited until she had set it on top of the stove before making his presence known.

   "Good morning."

   Amanda spun around. She took a deep breath. "How long have you been standing there? I thought you were still asleep."

   "How could anyone sleep with all the delicious smells coming from down here?"

   He walked over to the counter and poured a mug of coffee. "I see biscuits and I smelled the coffee and bacon, so I guess breakfast is almost ready. Do you want me to set the table or cook the eggs?"

   "Why don't you set the table."

   Amanda had not forgotten the events of the previous evening. She accepted Drew's assurance that he was not upset over their confrontations with Claire, but there was still the chance it would cause a permanent rift between him and his mother.

   When they had finished eating, Drew refilled both their mugs. Before sitting down, he pulled an envelope from the pocket of his robe and handed it to Amanda.

   "What's this?"

   "Open it."

   Looking wary, she did as he suggested. It contained two airline tickets to the Bahamas.

   "The honeymoon we never had," he explained. "I

An important message from the ARABESQUE Editor

Dear Arabesque Reader,

Because you've chosen to read one of our Arabesque romance novels, we'd like to say "thank you"! And, as a special way to thank you, we've selected four more of the books you love so well to send you for only $1.99.

Please enjoy them with our compliments, and thank you for continuing to enjoy Arabesque...the soul of romance.

Karen Thomas
Senior Editor,
Arabesque Romance Novels

SPECIAL OFFER!
4 BOOKS FOR ONLY $1.99

ARABESQUE
A PRODUCT OF
BET BOOKS

Check out our website at www.arabesquebooks.com

3 QUICK STEPS
TO RECEIVE YOUR "THANK YOU" GIFT
FROM THE EDITOR

Send back this card and you'll receive 4 Arabesque novels!
These books have a combined cover price of $20.00 or more,
but they are yours to keep for a mere $1.99.

There's no catch. You're under no obligation to buy anything.
We charge only $1.99 for the books (plus $1.50 for shipping
and handling, a total of $3.49). And you don't have to make
any minimum number of purchases—not even one!

We hope that after receiving your books you'll want to
remain an Arabesque subscriber. But the choice is yours to
continue or cancel, anytime at all! So why not take us up on
our invitation to receive 4 Arabesque Romance Novels, with
no risk of any kind. You'll be glad you did!

Call us
TOLL-FREE
at 1-888-345-BOOK

THE EDITOR'S "THANK YOU" GIFT INCLUDES:

- 4 books delivered for only $1.99 (plus $1.50 for shipping and handling)
- A FREE newsletter, *Arabesque Romance News*, filled with author interviews, book previews, special offers, and more!
- No risks or obligations. You're free to cancel whenever you wish... with no questions asked.

BOOK CERTIFICATE

Yes! Please send me 4 Arabesque books for $1.99 (+ $1.50 for shipping & handling, a total of $3.49). I understand I am under no obligation to purchase any books, as explained on the back of this card.

Name _____

Address _____ Apt. _____

City _____ State _____ Zip _____

Telephone ( ) _____

Signature _____

Offer limited to one per household and not valid to current subscribers. All orders subject to approval. Terms, offer, & price subject to change.

AN050A

Thank you!

Accepting the four introductory books for $1.99 (+ $1.50 for shipping & handling, a total of $3.49) places you under no obligation to buy anything. You may keep the books and return the shipping statement marked "cancel". If you do not cancel, about a month later we will send 4 additional Arabesque novels, and bill you a preferred subscriber's price of just $4.00 per title (plus a small shipping and handling fee). That's $16.00 for all 4 books for a savings of 33% off the cover price. You may cancel at any time, but if you choose to continue, every month we'll send you 4 more books, which you may either purchase at the preferred discount price. . . or return to us and cancel your subscription.

decided it had been delayed long enough and since Valentine's Day is just around the corner, I thought this would be the perfect time. What do you think?"

"Since I don't have a job yet, I guess this is a good time for it. The only problem is you didn't give me much time to prepare. This is less than a week away."

"Amanda, you're not upset about not having a job yet, are you?"

"Not really, just a little disappointed. That job at the mental health center seemed so promising."

"Sweetheart, you've had enough experience with government-funded agencies to know that this kind of thing isn't unusual. Didn't the director say that one of the other psychologists was leaving soon?"

"Yes, but that doesn't mean I'll get the job."

"You just sent another group of resumes out, right?"

"Yes, Drew."

"I know it's hard, but something will turn up. You're too good at what you do for that talent to go to waste."

"You really don't have to give me a pep talk. I know I'll find a job eventually. Meanwhile, I'm seriously considering volunteering at one of the centers." She smiled. "After the honeymoon, of course. For the next few days, I'll be too busy shopping."

Drew's prediction came true sooner than Amanda expected. Monday morning she received two telephone calls that would eliminate much of the leisure time she had enjoyed since reconciling with Drew.

The first call came soon after Drew had left for the office. It was from the director of one of the domestic violence shelters to which she had sent her resume.

"Hello, Ms. Connors, it's Joan Morris. I spoke with you a few weeks ago when I received your resume."

"Yes, Ms. Morris, I remember."

"I'm calling to see if you're still interested in a part-time position as a counselor. As I explained before, our current funding won't permit us to hire a full-time counselor, but one of our part-time psychologists has given notice."

"I'd be very interested in the position, Ms. Morris. The problem is that I'm going away in a few days. I'll be gone for a week."

"Would you be able to come in for an interview before you leave, say tomorrow?"

"Yes, I could arrange that."

They arranged a time for the interview. Ms. Morris assured her that it would be at least a week before she made her decision, so Amanda's trip would not interfere with her consideration for the position.

Amanda breathed a sigh of relief when she hung up the phone. She had to remind herself that she had not been hired yet, but it was the first call that had seemed promising.

Later that afternoon, she received a call from Maya's mother. "I'm sorry to bother you, Ms. Reynolds, but you said I should call if Maya wanted to talk to you."

Amanda overlooked the woman's use of her maiden name. It occurred to her that she might not even know her married name.

"Don't worry about that, Mrs. Phillips. Is Maya having a particular problem."

"No, I wouldn't say that. She still goes to see the counselor and she's been doing real good. She really loves those paints and things you gave her."

Amanda smiled. She recalled the handwritten note she had received from the child, thanking her for the set of paints and brushes.

"To tell you the truth, Ms. Reynolds, I think she just misses you. I know you're probably real busy, but she's been begging me to call you."

"I'll be glad to talk to her, Mrs. Phillips. In fact, I can give her a call later today. What would be a good time to call?"

"I guess around five-thirty. We'll be home by then and she'll have some time to talk before dinner. Is that a good time for you?"

"Five-thirty will be fine."

Amanda was on the telephone with Maya when Drew arrived home that evening. The child's mother appeared to be right, although a telephone conversation was not ideal for making a determination of progress. Then Amanda reminded herself that she was no longer Maya's counselor. Maya simply needed to be reassured that Amanda had not deserted her completely.

Drew entered the living room as she hung up the telephone. He leaned over the back of the chair where she was sitting and planted a kiss on her cheek.

"Hi, babe."

"Hi. I was just talking to Maya."

"Maya?"

"The child that had me so upset a couple of months ago."

"How is she?"

"She sounds good. Her mother says she's doing well."

"So, do you feel better about her now?"

She nodded. "Yes, I do, much better."

"Good. Did you go shopping today?"

"No, I decided I needed to inventory what I have before I buy anything else."

She stood up and came over to him, smiling. "I do have some good news, though. I have a job interview tomorrow."

He hugged her. "That's great. I knew your talent wouldn't go to waste."

"I don't have the job yet, Drew, but I love your vote of confidence."

After her interview the next day, Amanda learned that shopping was not going to be as easy as she thought. Although the store merchandise never coincided with the current season, it was a little early for them to have a large selection of spring and summer clothes in stock.

Amanda had summer clothes, but they were mostly work clothes; she had very few casual summer clothes. She had never taken a vacation—most of her time had been spent working, so she had very little use for casual clothes. After three days of scouring the department stores, she managed to assemble enough for a decent wardrobe. The one item she had been unable to find was a bathing suit.

It was evening when she returned to the house. She was pulling into the garage just as Drew drove up behind her. He pulled into the space beside her car. After closing the garage door, he joined her at the trunk of her car.

"How'd the job interview go?"

"Okay, I guess. They won't be making a decision before we return from the Bahamas."

Drew eyed the packages in the trunk of the car. "At least it seems you had a successful day shopping."

"Semi-successful. I still haven't found a bathing suit."

Drew grinned and gathered the bulk of the parcels in his arms. "Maybe we'll get lucky and find a private lagoon. I'm sure I'd enjoy skinny-dipping."

"I don't think I'd trust the chance of having that much privacy."

"Spoilsport. Don't worry about the bathing suit. I'm sure you'll be able to find one in the islands."

They entered the house and Drew carried the packages upstairs. Amanda displayed her purchases while he changed his clothes.

"Other than the bathing suit, I think I have more than enough outfits for the week."

"Good. I called Jennifer this afternoon. She said she'd pick up the mail and check the house while we're away."

The evening before their flight, they drove to a hotel at the airport. Spending the night close to the airport would be less hectic because of the very early morning departure.

Less than twenty-four hours later, they were being shown to a bungalow on Paradise Island. Drew carried the bags to the bedroom while Amanda explored the rooms.

The living room was furnished with a rattan-trimmed white sofa complemented by two chairs in a muted tropical print. The same print covered the chairs to the dinette set. There was a small kitchenette, separated from the dining area by a wet bar.

Drew returned from the bedroom as she opened the sliding glass doors to the balcony that extended to the bedroom. It overlooked a small lagoon surrounded by palm trees and flowering shrubs.

The resort was beautifully designed for privacy. They had been driven from the main building in a golf cart. Although they had passed other bungalows along the path, none were visible now.

He came up beside her and put his arm around her shoulder. "It really lives up to the brochure. I could be content to spend the next few months here with you, instead of only a week."

He took her in his arms. Amanda's arms entwined his neck. "That's not surprising, though. I'm content anywhere with you," he murmured seconds before his lips claimed hers.

Amanda was breathless when he finally broke the kiss. They stood there, holding each other for a long moment. Amanda was the first to speak.

"I guess we'd better go unpack."

"If you insist."

The bedroom was decorated in a similar print as the living room. The king-size bed was covered in a print bedspread, offset by the seafoam green carpet. Before unpacking, Amanda completed her tour. She discovered a large whirlpool tub in the bathroom, as well as a double-size shower stall.

After they unpacked and changed clothes, they strolled the path winding through the resort. The path led to a small beach and then circled back to the main building. After looking around the gift shop, they had dinner and then returned to the bungalow. Amanda turned to Drew as they entered the bedroom. Wrapping her arms around his waist, she gazed up at him.

"Care to join me in a nice bubble bath?" she asked, grinning.

"That's funny. I was thinking the same thing."

When they were immersed in the water, Drew pulled her close to his side. "I have a confession to make."

"And just what is this great confession?"

He lifted her onto his lap. His hands began smoothing the bubbles across her shoulders, as his fingers drew circles in the lather around her breasts.

"I keep discovering new and very interesting places to make love to you."

Amanda's eyes widened. Her throat went dry. "You can't mean what I think you mean."

Moments later, with her legs wrapped around his waist, she learned he meant exactly what she had guessed. His hands caressed her back and moved down to cup her buttocks. Amanda gasped in pleasure with his first thrust. Her body tensed, reaching for the ecstasy that she knew would come.

Drew strained in his efforts to prolong the sensations running through his body. He luxuriated in the feel of her skin sensuously slick against his own. He finally gave in to his body's craving for fulfillment.

They collapsed in each other's arms. Their hands continued to stroke each other's heated skin.

"I think we'd better get out of here before we fall asleep and drown." His words were punctuated by a chuckle.

"That would make quite a story. 'Two lovers found drowned in tub at resort'—it might ruin the resort's business."

Amanda yawned. "That would be a shame. It's such a beautiful resort," she said, never raising her head from where it rested against his chest.

"Since you're already half asleep, I guess it's up to me to get us out of here."

He eased her from his lap and lifted her out of the water. Setting her on the ledge surrounding the tub, he stood up and let the water out of the tub. Amanda was little help as he dried her and himself and carried her to bed. Within a few minutes, they were both sound asleep.

The rest of the week was much the same as the first afternoon. The day after their arrival, they went shopping. Amanda found a bathing suit, although she was skeptical that she would have the courage to wear it anyplace other than the secluded lagoon near their bungalow.

They spent their days swimming, walking the resort paths, and watching the sunsets. They talked, danced, and made love. Neither could have wished for a more perfect honeymoon. There was nothing to give Amanda any warning that her whole world was in danger of crashing down around her.

Twelve

The day after she and Drew returned from the Bahamas, Amanda received a telephone call from Mrs. Morris, offering her the position at the shelter. Amanda accepted the offer, and was scheduled to begin work the following Monday.

Her responsibilities would be more specialized than her previous assignments. She would be counseling children to help them overcome the effects of witnessing domestic violence. Other psychologists would be counseling those who were the actual victims of abuse.

Later that same evening, she received a call from Nicole. Her friend was a nurse at the hospital close by.

"Amanda, I called to let you know your father was admitted to the hospital last night. He was in a car accident. It's doesn't appear to be anything very serious. He has a mild concussion and a broken leg, but he's in traction, so he'll probably be here for a while."

When Nicole received no response from her friend, she continued, "Amanda, I know you're not interested in having any contact with him, but I thought you should know."

"Thanks, Nicole. I appreciate your calling to tell me. I can't promise I'll go to see him, but I'll think about it."

For the next few days she did just that: She thought about it. Drew noticed her preoccupation and mentioned it a few times, but she assured him that nothing was wrong.

The response she had received from her father when she called him a month earlier was still fresh in her mind. When her father had commented that he was not surprised she had come running back to her rich husband, Amanda had put an end to the conversation. Although his attitude was not as abusive as it had been in the past, he was far from pleasant.

She tried, now, to give him the benefit of the doubt. Maybe he had mellowed since the accident. Sometimes a close call has the effect of changing a person's attitude toward the people in his life, and life in general. She finally convinced herself that if she went to visit him, this encounter would be different.

After three days of mulling over the situation, she made up her mind that she had to go see him. Even though Nicole had said his injuries were not life-threatening, one could never be sure. If anything happened to him, she would regret not having tried to bridge the gap between them.

When Amanda entered the hospital, she had no idea where to go. She had considered calling Nicole, but she did not want to tell her friend she was coming. If the visit did not go well, she would rather keep it to herself.

After stopping at the information desk, she made her way to the elevator. The closer she came to her father's room, the more nervous she became. She finally reached the door, took a deep breath, and entered.

His eyes were closed and she took a moment to appraise his appearance. She wondered if Nicole had told her the truth. He did not look well at all. The intervening years had not been kind to him. He looked twenty years older than she remembered, rather than just eight.

He opened his eyes as she approached. She knew immediately from his expression that he was not one of those people who has a miraculous change of heart.

"What are you doing here?"

"I heard about the accident. I just came to see how you're doing."

"Well I hate to disappoint you, but the doctor says I'll be fine."

Amanda shook her head. "Dad, why would you say something like that? I've never wished for anything bad to happen to you. I came here to see if there was anything you need."

He grunted. "Oh, now that you got that rich husband back, you're here to hand out charity."

Amanda sighed. This was a waste of time and effort. "Drew's not rich and I'm only offering what I would to any friend or relative under these circumstances. Since you obviously don't want anything from me, I'll leave you in peace."

When she reached the door, she turned back to face him. "I hope you feel better soon."

When Amanda reached home, she was surprised that Drew was not there. She checked the messages, but there was nothing. Maybe he was on his way.

Two hours later, she had changed clothes, dinner was done, and there was still no sign of Drew. Another hour passed and she became worried that something had happened to him. By ten o'clock, her concern had turned to anger. She gave up on dinner, but could not bring herself to throw it away. Instead, she wrapped it up and placed it in the refrigerator.

She was halfway up the stairs to bed when Drew entered the hallway from the garage. She turned and looked at him when he greeted her. Giving no response, she turned away and continued up the stairs.

Drew frowned. She was obviously angry, although he had no idea why. He put his briefcase down, hung up his coat and followed his wife up the stairs.

Amanda was still seething when she exited the bathroom dressed in her gown and robe. Drew was seated on the bed. He had no intention of letting her go to bed without an explanation for her mood.

"Would you care to tell me why you're not speaking to me?"

Amanda glared at him. "I'd have been happy to speak to you on the phone if you had called to tell me you'd be late. I was worried that something had happened to you. I don't know what it is about men that they can't pick up a telephone and call to let someone know when they'll be late. It's a matter of common courtesy."

Drew was determined to stay calm. "Amanda, did you forget that I was teaching the workshop at the community college tonight? I thought I'd mentioned it to you a few weeks ago. If I didn't, I apologize."

Amanda turned away from him. She wanted to go through the floor. It had completely slipped her mind.

"Amanda?"

"You did mention it," she murmured, still unable to face him. "I'm sorry. I forgot."

"Why didn't you call me on the cell phone?"

She shrugged. "It never occurred to me."

Drew stood up and walked over to her. After turning her around to face him, he took her in his arms. He sensed there was more that she had not told him.

"Amanda, is there something else that's bothering you?"

Amanda tensed. "It's nothing."

Drew held her away from him and tipped her face up to look in her eyes. Amanda reluctantly met his gaze.

"If it has you this upset, it's not 'nothing'," he insisted.

Taking her hand, he led her over to the bed. Sitting down again, he urged her onto his lap.

"What is it, sweetheart?"

Amanda shook her head. "It really isn't anything, Drew. Not anything new anyway. Nicole called me a few days ago and told me my father had been admitted to the hospital. He'd been in a car accident. It's not serious, but I decided I should go and see him."

She sighed. "I had almost convinced myself that a close call like a car accident would change him. It didn't. He wasn't pleasant."

His hand stroked her back. "I'm sorry, baby. I wish you had told me. I wish you had let me go with you."

Amanda gazed up into his eyes. She placed her hand on the side of his face.

"I appreciate that, sweetheart, but you can't fight all my battles for me." She shrugged. "Besides, it wasn't a battle, really. Just a little unpleasantness."

"Are you planning to go back to see him again?"

"I don't know. I doubt it. He pretty much told me not to bother. If it hadn't been for Nicole, I probably wouldn't have gone at all."

"What did she tell you? I thought you said he wasn't seriously hurt."

"He wasn't. He has a concussion and a broken leg and he's in traction. Nicole just called because she thought I should know. I had to see him, to find out how he would react. I had to know if he had changed in his attitude toward me."

She stretched up and kissed his cheek. "Thanks, Drew."

"For what?"

"For being so sweet and caring, and patient."

"That's what husbands are for, isn't it?"

"Since you put it that way, I guess that goes for wives, too."

She began opening the buttons of his shirt. It fell open and she began caressing his chest. "Tell me, would what happened earlier be defined as an argument?"

"I wouldn't exactly call it an argument. I'd consider it more of a misunderstanding than an argument." He took a deep breath when her fingers grazed his nipples.

Amanda frowned. "That's too bad," she murmured into his ear before her teeth began nipping at his earlobe. Her hand moved to his waist and began easing down the zipper of his slacks.

"You want us to have an argument?"

Her hand slipped into the opening of his slacks. "Only because it would be so pleasant to make up afterward."

Drew chuckled as he untied the sash of her robe and slid his hand inside. Capturing an enticing breast in his hand, his thumb began teasing the already turgid nipple.

"Since when do we need the excuse of making up after an argument for what's obviously on your mind?"

If she had intended to respond to his question, he gave her no opportunity. His mouth came down on hers and she opened to his exploring tongue. Moments later, their clothing lay in heaps on the floor and they were locked in the timeless rhythm of love.

Two days after Amanda's visit to her father, she received another telephone call from Nicole. They chatted for a few minutes, catching up on the recent events in their lives. Finally, Nicole broached the subject that had prompted her call.

"Amanda, one of the clerks in the hospital business office approached me today after she discovered that I know your father. They're having a problem with the billing. He didn't have his car insurance information or his hospitalization card on him at the time of the accident, and the information he gave them from memory is incorrect. They'd like for you to call them."

"I don't know what help I can be. You know I wouldn't have the information they need. Didn't you tell them that?"

"I did try to tell them, but I think they're hoping you'll be able to get it."

Amanda hesitated. She did not want to become any more involved in her father's business.

"I know it's an inconvenience, Amanda, but he hasn't been much help."

"Do they have to have the information now? Why can't he just call them when he's discharged and give them the information?"

"Because their experience has been that after some patients are discharged, they become very lax about helping the hospital get paid. For them, it's not a priority. Of course, without the information, they would simply bill him for the entire amount. Too many times, that still doesn't ensure that the hospital gets the information."

Amanda had no idea what other patients would do. She guessed that her father would be one of those who might not be very cooperative. For him, threatening to have the delinquent bill put on his credit report would mean nothing.

"Alright, Nicole, I'll call them tomorrow and see what I can do."

"Thanks."

Amanda hung up the telephone and sighed. There

was some doubt that she would be able to help. She could not imagine her father would give his permission for her to go into his house to get the information needed. More than that, she could not imagine asking his permission. She still had her house key, but for all she knew, he might have changed the locks. But she would call the hospital business office as she promised Nicole.

Amanda did not tell Drew of this latest development. She had to handle this alone. Drew had already had more than enough involvement with her father. If he knew she planned to go to her father's house, he would insist on accompanying her. Her father would probably be angry enough with her for what he would consider snooping. If he found out Drew had been with her, he would be livid.

When Amanda called the business office the next day, the clerk apologized for the inconvenience. "We don't know any other way to get the information, Mrs. Connors. It's important that we have the information from both insurances. There are some tests the doctor wants to order and we need to know if his hospitalization will cover it or if it should be billed to the automobile insurance."

"I'll see what I can do. I won't have an opportunity to check on it before this weekend."

"That's fine. I'd appreciate anything you can do to help."

Thirteen

Saturday morning, Amanda prepared to go to her former home. She did not tell Drew her plans. Friday evening, she had mentioned casually that she was going to visit Maya the next day. There was no need to tell him she would be making another stop before going to Chester.

She left shortly after breakfast and reluctantly drove to her father's house. After parking at the curb, she rummaged in her purse for the house key. It had required a bit of searching the previous evening before she found it stashed away in the back of her jewelry box.

After she left her father's house eight years earlier, she realized it had never been a happy home. She and her father had moved into the house when she was nine years old. They had lived in an apartment for two years in Philadelphia, where they had moved soon after her mother died.

She vaguely remembered happy times before her mother became ill. Life with her father had been tolerable for a few years, although he had never been affectionate. It was not until she became a teenager and began socializing that he became abusive.

The few times she had dated, she endured such accusations and reproach that she soon ceased dating at all. His moods were so unpredictable that she slowly withdrew from most of her friends. Nicole was the only one who had clung to their friendship.

It was the times she spent in the company of Nicole's family that really opened her eyes. The relationship between Nicole and her parents was loving and affectionate, and they included Amanda in that circle of love.

As a teenager, seeing the affection between Nicole's parents had sparked an unpleasant memory. Her own parents' relationship had never been affectionate. There had always been a certain tension in the air. She had felt it, even as a young child.

When she began studying psychology, she had naturally thought about her own childhood and adolescence. For years before that, she had told herself that her father, like many men, was simply not demonstrative.

As unpleasant as the truth was, her studies and further introspection had finally led her to the conclusion that her father hated her, or at least his feelings for her were far from loving.

As she walked toward the house, she took notice of the property's deterioration. The sidewalk was cracked in several places. The porch, front door, and window frames were badly in need of painting. Why had he let the house fall into such a bad state of disrepair?

Amanda climbed the porch stairs and opened the storm door that creaked on rusty hinges. The key fit into the lock with ease. The locks had not been changed.

For a few years before she left home, she'd suspected that her father was drinking too much. Considering the deterioration of the outside of the house, she wondered if his drinking had gotten totally out of control.

When she entered, she had even more reason to suspect that that was the case. The house was not unlivable, but the disarray was not the result of a few days', or even a few weeks' neglect.

She made her way to the old desk in the living room. She remembered he had always kept important papers and bills in its various drawers and cubbyholes. As she searched through the desk for the information she needed, she found the answer to some of her questions. It was a letter dated three years earlier, dismissing him from his job as a court bailiff.

That piece of information raised the question as to how he had managed financially for the past three years. Shuffling through the haphazardly stored papers, she came across a recent pay stub from a private security company.

She had gained some insight into her father's decline and his current situation, but she still had not found the information she needed. Further exploration finally revealed one of the objects of her search. She discovered the premium payment notice for her father's hospitalization insurance. It was not clear if the premium had been paid or if the insurance was active, but at least it would provide the name of the company and the policy numbers for the hospital to get the information they needed. Now, if she could find the car insurance policy or statement, her task would be completed.

She tried to open the last drawer, but it was stuck. It appeared that papers or something else was jamming it. She applied a great deal of force in her efforts to loosen it and the drawer fell out of her hands, scattering its contents on the floor around her.

She found the insurance policy among the pile of papers and was gathering the remaining papers when one letter caught her attention. She picked it up, briefly noting the hospital letterhead. It was addressed to her father and signed by a doctor. The doctor was requesting, almost begging, her father to visit her mother in the hospital. He explained that he believed a show of concern and support would be beneficial to his patient.

Amanda's gaze returned to the letterhead. The hospital was a mental institution. Her mother had been a mental patient, and her father had written her off. The lump that formed in her throat was nothing compared to the shock she received when she read the date on the letter. The letter had been written two years after her mother was supposed to have died!

Amanda stumbled to a chair and sat down, staring at the words that had become a blur. She now understood why she had not been allowed to attend her mother's "funeral." Her father's explanation had been that she was too young, that it would not be good for her.

She also understood why they had moved to Philadelphia less than six months after her mother's supposed death and again two years later. It seemed the doctor's letter had prompted the second move. Once her father had decided to eliminate her mother from their lives, he did not want periodic reminders of her existence.

She closed her eyes, trying to will back the tears that had already formed in them. Taking a deep breath, she forced her emotions under control. She began searching for other clues.

Was her mother still alive? If so, where was she now? Had she been searching for her child all these years? When her father uprooted them the second time, had it been not only to prevent the doctor's letters from reaching him, but a deliberate effort to keep her mother from finding them?

Amanda examined each piece of paper as she replaced them in the drawer. There was an earlier letter from the same doctor. Why had her father bothered to save them?

The answer to that question was partially explained by the only other important document among the papers. It was a divorce decree, citing her mother's mental condition as the basis for the petition. So, he had ruthlessly severed all ties with the woman for whom he must have, at one time, professed love. "In sickness and in health" obviously had no meaning for him.

The shock and pain she had experienced upon her initial discovery were rapidly being replaced by anger and determination. She wrote down the hospital and doctor's name and telephone numbers. She also jotted down the insurance information that had been the reason for the visit.

After replacing the drawer, she looked around to assure herself that the room was as it had been when she had entered. Considering the overall condition of the house, it was unlikely he would notice if the room was not in the same condition as he had left it.

She let herself out and locked the door behind her. A few minutes later, she was in her car and headed for Chester. She had promised Maya a visit today. Her personal problems were no excuse for disappointing the child. She had already had too many disappointments in her young life.

Drew noticed that Amanda seemed preoccupied for the remainder of the weekend. When he mentioned it to her, she dismissed his concern. Her excuse of trying to get back into the routine of work did not entirely ease his worry, but he did not persist with his questions. He recalled her plan to visit Maya. Although she was not as distressed as she had been over the abused child months earlier, he asked her about the visit. Her response told him she had enjoyed seeing her former patient. There was no reason to believe that visit was responsible for her strange mood.

Her attitude toward him was no different. It was that assurance that gave him the patience to wait for her to work through the problem. He knew her well enough to believe that in time, she would either cope with the problem herself, or the reason for her mood would be revealed.

When she and Drew attended church on Sunday, Amanda regained a semblance of her former peace of mind. She was determined to learn the truth about her mother, but the anger she had felt toward her father abated to a small degree.

She accepted the probability that she would never understand her father's motives or the reasons for most of his actions. That did not concern her since she no longer had to cope with his treatment of her. She would not allow him to steal the happiness she had found.

Monday morning, before leaving for her job at the shelter, Amanda called the hospital billing office and gave them the insurance information they had requested.

She was anxious to try the number she had obtained from the letter concerning her mother, but it was not a call she wanted to make from work. Her attempt to contact the hospital would have to wait until the next day.

Early Tuesday morning, she placed the call to the mental hospital where her mother had been a patient. When the operator answered, she asked to be connected to Dr. Ormond. There was a moment's hesitation before the operator replied.

"I'm sorry, but there's no doctor here by that name. Perhaps someone else can help you."

"I guess I really need to talk to someone in your patient information office."

"What is it in reference to?"

"I'm trying to locate my mother. I know she was a patient there some years ago. If I could obtain the address you have for her in your files, it might be helpful."

"I'm sorry, but I don't think we're permitted to give you that information."

Amanda was not surprised to hear that. "In that case, would you have any idea how I could contact Dr. Ormond? Evidently, he was on staff there at one time. I have a letter from him that indicates he was her doctor when she was a patient there."

"I'm sorry. I can connect you with our records office, but with all the changes that have taken place here, I'm not sure they'll even have that information."

The operator transferred the call. Just as she had indicated, the records office was of no help. They, in turn, transferred her to the personnel office. When Amanda explained that the letter was more than fifteen years old, she could almost hear the disgust in the clerk's voice.

"I'm sorry, but records that old aren't even stored in this facility. Unless the doctor was on staff here in the past five years, I can't help you."

Amanda finally hung up the telephone, thoroughly disgusted and dismayed. There had to be a way to get an address for her mother. On the heels of that thought came a more upsetting possibility. If her mother had been living with her father when she was admitted to the hospital, it was likely that that was the only address they would have in their files.

The rest of the day, she reflected on the possibility that she might never find her mother. She finally, determinedly, pushed that thought aside. If she had no other option, she would go to the hospital and beg them for the address in her mother's file. There was always the possibility she had given them some other address when she was discharged, especially if she had received outpatient treatment.

On Wednesday, Amanda had little time to think about her discovery. Even if any possibilities had come to mind, she had no time to act on them. Her counseling duties at the shelter kept her busy all day.

It was not until late Thursday that the telephone directory occurred to her as a possible source of the information she sought. If her mother had been hospitalized for two years, it was unlikely that she had returned to their old address. That did not mean she had left the area. She dialed Information, but there was no listing for an Elizabeth Reynolds. She stifled her feelings of disappointment when that attempt proved fruitless.

Her idea of locating her mother through the simple means of using the telephone directory had not been totally useless. It led to the notion that she might have better luck locating the doctor by that method.

Friday morning she put her idea to the test. The new telephone information systems proved very helpful. The operator located a Dr. Ralph Ormond, psychiatrist, in an affluent community in nearby Montgomery County.

It had to be the right person. How many psychiatrists named Ralph Ormond could there be in Philadelphia or its suburbs? She dialed the number with shaking fingers. The voice that answered identified itself as the answering service.

Amanda was a little disappointed, but she left a message indicating she was a relative of one of the doctor's patients. She told herself she was not lying; she had simply neglected to mention that the relative was not a recent patient.

Later that evening, Amanda accepted the fact that she would have to endure another weekend of waiting and hoping. The doctor had not returned her call. She had refused to leave the name of the relative. It was Saturday and he had no reason to believe the call was urgent. She reminded herself to be patient, as Drew had been patient with her.

She had seen the concern on Drew's face. She knew he had not believed her explanation for her strange mood. He wanted to help, but she could not tell him the truth, not yet. She had to find her mother first. Once she located her mother, she would explain everything.

On Sunday morning, Drew awakened to the strong smell of coffee. Upon opening his eyes, he understood why the smell was so strong. Amanda had just entered the room with a tray.

"Good morning."

"Morning," he responded, rising from the bed and walking toward her.

"You're supposed to stay in bed. That's the idea of breakfast in bed."

He took the tray from her. "No problem," he insisted, carrying the tray to the bench at the foot of the bed instead of the sitting area.

He pulled back the covers and patted the bed. "I hope you're planning to join me."

She picked up the tray. "Gladly, but since this is my treat, you get in first."

"Are we going to chance actually eating in bed this time?"

"Why not? The sheets are washable."

She placed the tray across his lap and walked around to the other side of the bed. After sliding across the wide expanse, she propped the pillows against the headboard and settled down beside him.

Drew poured coffee for both of them. After a few sips, they took turns feeding each other tidbits of bacon, boiled eggs and fresh strawberries. There was one strawberry left when Amanda eased away from him and rose from the bed.

She came around to his side of the bed and reached for the tray. She started toward the door, but he called her back. She set the tray down on the bench once again.

"I think I'll have that last strawberry."

She picked it up with her fingers and brought it to him. "Open up," she instructed.

When she placed it in his mouth, his lips closed around her fingers. His hand reached over and tugged at the sash on her robe. It fell open, revealing her nude body. He slid his arm around her waist, drawing her down onto his lap. After quickly disposing of the robe, he eased her onto her back. His lips met hers, his eager tongue seeking entrance to the sweet nectar within.

Much too soon he lifted his head, murmuring, "You taste like strawberries."

His lips claimed hers once again, hungrily this time. His fingers traced a line across her collarbone and down to her breast. A moment later, his lips followed the same route his fingers had taken, planting feather-light kisses on her heated skin. His hand continued stroking her body, coming to rest at the juncture of her thighs.

Amanda moaned and parted her legs in response to his questing fingers. Her hands roamed over his body, first caressing the flexing muscles of his back and then moving lower to stroke his firm buttocks. She tightened her arms around his waist, pulling him closer.

Drew settled in between her soft, silky thighs. His shaft pressed against the soft curls where his hand had rested moments earlier. With his first thrust, her legs encircled his waist and her hands clutched his shoulders. Soon they were engaged in passion's intoxicating rhythm.

Later, they lay quietly savoring the aftermath of sated desire. Amanda sighed contentedly. Whatever came of her search for her mother, she would not allow it to destroy the happiness she had found with Drew. She was startled when he spoke. It was almost as if he had read her mind.

His hands gently stroked her back as he murmured, "Amanda, I know something's been bothering you. I won't press you to tell me what it is. I just want you to remember that I'm here for you, to help you through whatever problems come up." He kissed her temple. "That's what husbands are for, remember?"

Amanda stretched up to kiss the corner of his mouth. "I remember, Drew. I love you."

It was not what he had wanted to hear, but he accepted it. He would continue to be patient.

Fourteen

On Monday, when she arrived home from the shelter, there was a message from Dr. Ormond waiting for her. She called the doctor's office, but as she expected, was only able to contact the answering service. She left another message.

Tuesday morning, Amanda planned to attempt to contact Dr. Ormond again. Before that opportunity came, she received the call she had been anticipating, and fearing would never come. She had tried to prepare herself for the possibility that contacting Dr. Ormond would put her no closer to finding her mother. After all, her other attempts had been unsuccessful. All her hopes were pinned on this man, who was the only link she had.

"Mrs. Connors, this is Dr. Ormond. I received the message that you wanted to speak to me about a relative."

"That's right. I think I owe you an apology, though. The relative is not a current patient of yours. It's my mother, Elizabeth Reynolds. She was a patient of yours many years ago when she was hospitalized. You were on staff at the hospital and you wrote a letter to my father."

There was an uncomfortable silence on the other end of the telephone. She could imagine what he was thinking, a strange woman calling him out of the blue about a patient he had treated more than fifteen years ago.

"I suppose this is rather unbelievable. I only recently found the letter you wrote to my father."

"Miss Reynolds, I'm sorry, Mrs. Connors, why are you calling me now? That must have been ten years ago."

"Until recently, when I found the letter, I thought my mother was dead. Do you remember anything that might help me?"

"Mrs. Connors, can you come to my office? I might have some information, but you must understand that I can't give you any information over the telephone."

Amanda's heart beat faster. "I understand. I'll be glad to come to your office. When would be a good time?"

"Actually, I have some time early this afternoon, around two-thirty."

Amanda wrote down the directions. He must know something. Otherwise, he would simply have told her he had no information.

Amanda took a deep breath and opened the door to Dr. Ormond's office. A few minutes later, she was seated in a comfortable chair in front a balding, gray-haired man who had one of the kindest faces she had ever seen.

"I can't imagine anyone else wanting to know about my mother, but I understand your position, Dr. Ormond."

She removed two documents from her purse and placed them on the desk. "I brought my birth certificate and marriage certificate."

"That's not really necessary, Mrs. Connors. I'd like to know more about this letter you found, though."

"Please call me Amanda. I won't go into the whole story, but in searching through some of my father's papers I found a letter you had written, asking him to visit my mother. My father told me my mother died before I was eight years old, and your letter was dated two years after that."

She explained the steps she had taken in an effort to locate her mother. "You were my last resort. I guess I hoped that you had continued to treat her as an outpatient and would have an address for her after she left the hospital."

"Amanda, I'm a psychiatrist and I hate to admit it, but I don't know any way to tell you this except to say it straight out. When your mother was discharged from the hospital, she was sent to another institution."

"What kind of institution?"

"It's similar to a nursing home, but for the mentally ill. When the state began closing the large hospitals, many of the long-term patients were sent either to group homes or to these institutions. She's no longer officially my patient, but I have visited her from time to time."

"Are you telling me she never recovered?"

"I'm afraid not. She was still at the home when I visited her six months ago. Even though she's no longer my patient, I've maintained contact with her."

He took a slip of paper from the desk and wrote some information on it. He passed it to her.

"That's the name of the home and the address. I suggest you call first. Ask to speak to Mrs. Lindhurst."

"What's wrong with my mother, Dr. Ormond?"

"Your mother experienced a mental breakdown after her child was stillborn. She completely withdrew. With some coaxing and help from the nurses, she takes care of her physical needs, but that's about all. She lives in her own world."

"Isn't there anything that can be done for her? What about medication? With all the new drugs, it's hard to believe she can't be helped."

"The doctors, including myself, tried everything. It's as though her brain deliberately shut down. She didn't respond to any of the treatments or medications."

He rubbed his chin. "Perhaps I shouldn't mention it, but at one point, the doctors even considered the possibility that her behavior was a sham."

"You mean they thought she was faking her illness? What possible reason would she have for that?"

"None, that I could imagine. I suppose they were simply grasping at any idea that would explain their inability to reach her. We doctors tend to be reluctant to admit failure."

"Is she allowed to have visitors?"

"I don't see why not. I have to warn you, though. She probably won't know you." He hesitated.

"Is there something more, Dr. Ormond?"

"You mentioned that your father told you your mother had died. What did the rest of your family say?"

Amanda shrugged. "I have no other family that I'm aware of."

"What about neighbors?"

"As I recall, no one really bothered much with us. We moved six months later, so the new neighbors knew nothing about us. At the time, I didn't really think much about the neighbors. As I told you, I wasn't even eight years old when he told me she had died. Naturally, I wouldn't think he was lying to me."

He nodded. "I'm very sorry, Amanda. I wish I had better news for you."

"Thank you, Dr. Ormond. I appreciate your seeing me."

When Amanda left the doctor's office, her first inclination was to go directly to see her mother. After some consideration, she reluctantly decided to wait. If she went now, she might not be home until late, and she was not prepared to reveal her discovery to Drew. Thursday would have to be soon enough.

As she drove home, Amanda forced herself to face the significance of the doctor's information. It was almost too much to handle. To have discovered, after all these years, that her mother was alive and then to learn that finding her might mean nothing after all. No, she would not allow herself to think that way.

Even if her mother had no memory of her, it would be enough to see her again. There was also the glimmer of hope that seeing her daughter would spark some memory. However unlikely after all these years, Amanda had to hold onto that hope.

Amanda made it through Wednesday with some difficulty. A full schedule of appointments kept her too busy for her mind to dwell on the prospects of her anticipated visit to the home where her mother now lived. The possible outcome of that visit was never completely out of her mind, though.

On Thursday morning, when Drew questioned if she had any plans for the day, she told him she planned to do some shopping. She was still in the process of redecorating, so he would not think it strange if she returned with no purchases to show for her outing.

She called the nursing home soon after he left for

the office. She asked to be connected with Mrs. Lindhurst, as Dr. Ormond had suggested.

"Mrs. Lindhurst speaking. May I help you?"

"Yes, my name is Amanda Connors. I understand my mother, Elizabeth Reynolds, is a patient there."

There was a moment of silence before Mrs. Lindhurst replied. "Yes, she is. You've never been here before?"

"No, I just recently learned the whereabouts of my mother. Dr. Ormond was her doctor years ago. When I located him, he told me she had been transferred to your facility."

"As a matter of fact, he's been here to visit her a few times."

"Dr. Ormond suggested I call before I come. I'd like to come visit her today. Are there any special visiting hours?"

"Under the circumstances, I think we can make an exception. If you tell me what time you expect to arrive, I'll make the arrangements."

The drive took almost an hour. Amanda arrived at the nursing home and after parking her car, she got out and looked around. From the outside, it seemed pleasant enough. The low brick building was surrounded by a small grassy area. There were a few benches scattered around, empty at the moment. It was not quite spring and there was a bit of a chill in the air.

She entered the lobby and was again relieved at the pleasant surroundings. The clerk looked up as she neared the desk.

"May I help you?"

"My name is Amanda Connors. I'm here to visit my mother, but I'm not sure where to find her."

"Yes, Mrs. Connors. Mrs. Lindhurst informed us that you would be arriving. If you'll have a seat, I'll let her know you're here."

Amanda took a seat and picked up a magazine. She flipped the pages, but was not really seeing the words.

Ten minutes later a tall, middle-aged woman approached her. "Mrs. Connors?"

Amanda rose from her chair. "Yes?"

The older woman extended her hand. "I'm Mrs. Lindhurst."

They shook hands. "I think it might be good for us to have a chat before I take you to see your mother."

Mrs. Lindhurst led her to a small office at the rear of the lobby area. "Have a seat, Mrs. Connors."

When Amanda was seated, the other woman continued. "You said on the phone that you only recently learned the whereabouts of your mother."

Amanda repeated the information she had given to Dr. Ormond, including the fact that she had believed her mother was dead. She also informed her that Dr. Ormond had explained her mother's condition.

"In that case, Mrs. Connors, you must be aware that your mother may not recognize you. In fact, there's every reason to believe she won't recognize you, or remember you."

"Yes, Dr. Ormond warned me about that possibility."

"There's more. Your mother sometimes has lucid moments when she's aware of what you're saying to her, but it takes quite a bit of coaxing before she responds. More often, there's no response or even an indication that she understands what you're saying."

"I understand."

Mrs. Lindhurst nodded. She rose from her chair and came around the desk.

"In that case, let's go see your mother."

She led Amanda through the lobby and down a hall to a large room filled with patients and a few nurse's aides. As she looked around the room, Amanda saw a middle-aged woman with short, mixed-gray hair sitting in a chair near the window. She sat perfectly still, her hands folded in her lap, looking out on the empty lawn.

Amanda's heartbeat quickened. It was her mother. It had been more than eighteen years, but she remembered her face. She would never forget that sweet, gentle face.

She followed Mrs. Lindhurst, weaving their way through the few tables scattered about. When they reached her mother Mrs. Lindhurst murmured her name. The woman looked up. In spite of the warnings, the blank expression on her mother's face nearly brought tears to Amanda's eyes.

"I have a visitor for you, Elizabeth," Mrs. Lindhurst said, indicating Amanda.

There was no response. Elizabeth looked at Amanda for a moment and then turned her attention back to the view outside the window.

"I'm sorry, Mrs. Connors. This is obviously not one of her better days."

Amanda shrugged. "Is it alright if I just sit here with her?"

"Certainly. You might even talk to her. She may not respond or give any sign that she understands, but it couldn't hurt."

Amanda did as she suggested. She spent the next two hours sitting with her mother. She held an intermittent one-sided conversation, relating the bits and pieces that she recalled from her childhood. At twelve-thirty, the aide came to lead her mother away for lunch.

"You're welcome to wait in the lobby, if you like."

"Maybe I'll go and have some lunch myself and come back later. Would that be alright?"

"That'll be fine. She should be finished with lunch in an hour."

Amanda returned as promised and spent two more hours chatting to her unresponsive mother. She reminded herself that it was only her first visit. In time, she might elicit some reaction.

Fifteen

For the next two weeks, Amanda followed the same routine. Every Tuesday and Thursday, she visited her mother. It was always the same. She chatted about anything and everything, but there was still no response.

Evelyn entered the lobby of the nursing home and looked around. She had been away for two weeks, but she did not expect there had been any change in the situation. It was later than her usual visiting time, and it appeared the patients had already been taken to lunch.

There was another visitor sitting in the lobby, evidently awaiting the patients' return. When the young woman looked up, it took all of Evelyn's control not to react. It was incredible! She was the spitting image of her father! The resemblance had not been so pronounced when she was a young child, but there was no question now.

Where had she been all these years? Why had she taken so long to come? Why had she bothered to come at all? Evelyn's instinctive reaction was reproach, but she immediately stifled that response. Amanda had only been a child when James took her away. Evelyn had no idea what he had told her about her mother.

It had to be difficult, to say the least, for Amanda to see her mother in her present mental state. For whatever reason she had avoided coming, she was here now. That was all that mattered. That, and the fact that it gave Evelyn an opportunity she had considered hopeless.

Amanda noticed the older woman who had paused near the door, evidently another visitor. She must be a new visitor or she would have chosen a better time for her arrival. Her mother and the other patients had left for lunch just a few minutes earlier. They would not return to the community room for another hour.

She spoke when the other woman joined her in the waiting area. "You just missed the patients. They've been taken to lunch."

"I was afraid of that. I stopped to do a bit of shopping and the time got away from me. It doesn't matter, though. I'm in no hurry."

She held out her hand. "I'm Evelyn Reed. I haven't seen you here before. Are you visiting someone, too?"

"Amanda Connors," she replied, shaking Evelyn's hand. "Yes, I'm visiting my mother."

"I'm sorry to hear that, dear. I can imagine it's very difficult for you. I've been coming here for quite a few years, visiting a dear friend of mine. I haven't seen you here before."

Amanda hesitated. "I've only been coming for a few weeks."

The two women chatted for a while. Evelyn asked a few subtle questions and learned that she lived in Philadelphia with her husband. She also learned that Amanda was a psychologist.

"I suppose that's somewhat of a help in coping with a situation such as this."

The look on Amanda's face hinted that she had gone too far. "I'm sorry, Amanda. I'm not trying to belittle the distress you're probably feeling. There were times, in my younger days, that I was accused of talking too much. I thought I had overcome that tendency."

"It's alright Mrs. Reed."

"If you'd rather not talk about it, please just say so. Sometimes it helps, but if you're uncomfortable with discussing your mother's condition, I understand."

"It's not that I'm uncomfortable. It's just that I'm still getting used to the situation. You see, she doesn't even know me and that's very difficult to handle."

A short time later, the patients returned to the community room. Evelyn followed Amanda into the room. She watched her for a few minutes as she conducted her one-sided conversation with her mother. She finally retreated without a word.

Amanda joined her mother near her seat at the window. A few minutes later, she looked around for Mrs. Reed. The other woman was nowhere in sight. Maybe her friend had not returned to the community room and she was visiting her in her room. Amanda shrugged off her questions concerning her new acquaintance and turned back to her mother to continue her usual monologue.

Mrs. Reed was at the nursing home for the next two weeks when Amanda visited, and they fell into the routine of having lunch together. After the first few shared lunches, Amanda felt herself drawn to the older woman.

When Amanda asked about her family, Evelyn told her she had been a widow for more than ten years. She readily answered her other questions until she asked where she currently lived. She answered vaguely that she lived in a small suburb close by. It had occurred to her that Amanda might think it too coincidental that she lived in the town where Amanda had lived as a child.

"Do you remember when I met you, you said you'd sometimes been accused of talking too much?"

Evelyn nodded.

"That's not true. At the time it was difficult to talk about my mother. It's not so difficult now, or maybe it's you. I don't know why I feel so comfortable confiding in you. Maybe I just needed someone to confide in and you're such a good listener."

"Haven't you confided in your husband?"

The older woman's question evoked a twinge of guilt. She had been practicing this deception for weeks, but she could not bring herself to tell Drew the truth.

"Amanda?"

Amanda's attention was focused on the ring, twisting it around on her finger. "No, I haven't."

Evelyn suspected her young friend was not entirely comfortable with that omission. She wondered what kind of man she had married that she would not tell him about her mother's condition.

"You see, until a few months ago, I thought my mother had died when I was seven years old." She toyed with the food remaining on her plate and continued to explain the move to Philadelphia and her discovery of the letter that had led her to her mother.

Evelyn's disgust and anger were evident in her expression. She had known that James Reynolds was a spiteful man, but to allow her to believe her mother was dead all these years was unforgivable. When Amanda looked up from her plate, the anger had been erased from the older woman's expression. Amanda gazed into the serene face across the table.

"This probably sounds really strange, but you remind of someone."

For a moment, Evelyn's heart beat faster, but she set her fears aside. It was just Amanda's imagination and, maybe, her need for a confidante.

"I probably just have one of those faces. You know how people are always saying each of us has a twin somewhere."

"I guess you're right."

During her fourth week of visits, Amanda experienced a small breakthrough. She entered the community room after lunch to join her mother at her usual spot by the window. When she neared her mother's chair, the older woman looked up and smiled.

"Amanda," she murmured.

A lump formed in Amanda's throat. She started to hug her mother, but something in Elizabeth's eyes stopped her. She knew then that her mother had called her name because she recognized her as a regular visitor, nothing more. She was not ready for any display of affection.

In spite of the minor improvement in her mother's condition, it was becoming increasingly difficult for Amanda to maintain her busy schedule. The physical part of it was no more than she had endured at times in the past. The emotional toll added to it made the difference. It was only a matter of time before she would have to tell Drew, and she had no idea what kind of reaction to expect from him, and his family.

She was reminded of this problem when he informed her that they had been invited to Easter dinner with his parents. She could imagine his mother's response if she knew of her mother's illness.

Easter dawned as a beautiful, sunny spring day. She and Drew had planned to attend the church service and then go directly to his parents' home.

Amanda stood in front of the mirror, checking her image for the tenth time. She was wearing a pale peach linen suit. Mother-of-pearl buttons complemented the short, double-breasted jacket. The short knife-pleated skirt ended just above her knees. Pearl earrings, and ivory pumps and clutch bag completed the simple outfit.

Drew came up behind her, leaned over and kissed her cheek. "You look beautiful, sweetheart." He looked at his watch. "And we'd better get going. You know what the church is like on Easter Sunday."

The church service gave Amanda the peace she anticipated needing to survive the afternoon. Later, at dinner, she was unsure if it was the church service or if Claire was actually less aggravating than usual. In fact, she came close to being pleasant.

Claire had had a lot of time to consider her husband's warning and reproach. She was determined to hold her tongue and observe her son and his wife more closely. She wanted to see what it was that convinced her husband of their feelings for each other.

At the end of the afternoon, Claire was forced to admit that her husband might have some basis for his convictions. Amanda was not a clinging vine, but when she looked at Drew, there was a tenderness in her expression. Aside from that, she noticed something else in her daughter-in-law's demeanor. She could not decide if it was worry or exhaustion. She could not imaging any reason for Amanda to be so exhausted that it would be evident in her appearance.

Claire was not the only one who was aware of the subtle change in Amanda. It was obvious she was troubled, and Drew was finding it more and more difficult to hold his tongue. He had broached the subject and she insisted she was only having some difficulty adjusting after being on hiatus from work for almost two months.

Drew was not convinced. Two months' hiatus did not seem long enough to require a great deal of adjustment. There was also the fact that she had been on the job for more than a month and was only working part-time. The information he had gleaned from their conversations told him that that alone was quite a change from her previous strenuous schedule.

He did not press her for a better explanation. He simply assured her that he was there for her support if there was a problem. There was no more he could do, at the moment.

The Tuesday after Easter, Amanda received another blow to her emotions. When she arrived at the nursing home, she was informed that Mrs. Lindhurst wished to speak with her. She was shown to the director's office.

"Come in and have a seat, Mrs. Connors."

When Amanda was seated, Mrs. Lindhurst took a deep breath. She opened a folder on her desk and perused the papers before she spoke.

"You don't know how deeply I regret having to give you the information I received yesterday. Your mother recently began experiencing severe headaches. The doctor has been to see her several times in relation to the problem. He finally ordered a CAT scan last week.

"I didn't mention this sooner because I didn't want to worry you unnecessarily. The test revealed an inoperable malignant brain tumor."

Amanda stared at her for a moment, unable to speak. She shook her head.

"This can't be happening. Why wasn't it found sooner?"

"Strangely enough, until the headaches, there was no indication of any real physical problems. She's always required some urging to handle her physical needs. Her hesitancy and awkwardness were taken as symptoms of her mental condition. For the most part, your mother has enjoyed very good physical health in the entire time she's been with us."

"You said the tumor is inoperable. What about radiation or chemotherapy?"

"That's the other reason I called you in here. As her closest relative, it's your decision as to where we go from here. Before you make that decision, I'm sure you'll want to speak with her doctor. I've told him about you and that I would be speaking with you today. His office isn't far from here. If you like, I'll call and see if he's available to see you today."

Amanda nodded. She was still trying to digest the shocking news she had just received, when Mrs. Lindhurst ended her telephone call.

"Dr. Aikens can see you at twelve-thirty." She wrote some information on a slip of paper and passed it to Amanda.

"That's his address."

Amanda stared blankly at the slip of paper.

"I'm sorry, Mrs. Connors. If there's anything I can do to help, please don't hesitate to ask."

"Thank you. Is my mother here?"

"Yes, she's in the community room, as usual."

Amanda stood at the door of the room for a moment, watching her mother. She became aware of the tears rolling down her cheeks when one of the aides approached her.

"Are you alright, miss?"

Amanda quickly wiped her eyes. "Not really."

"Is there something I can get you?"

"No, but thank you. I just have to get myself together. It won't do for her to see me like this."

The aide pointed across the room. "There's a ladies' room over there."

Amanda nodded and made her way through the tables. After washing her face, she scrutinized her image in the mirror. Satisfied that she had removed all traces of distress, she reentered the room and joined her mother.

Amanda sat across the desk from Dr. Aikens, listening to a report that held little assurance for her mother's recovery. She strained for some thread of hope, some reason to order the difficult and exhausting treatments.

"What you seem to be saying, Dr. Aikens, is that the only treatment you recommend is radiation."

He nodded. "That's the usual procedure in cases like your mother's. There will be some side effects, but there's a chance we can shrink the tumor."

"What kind of success can be expected with radiation?"

"I'm afraid I can't offer you any assurances. The tumor may or may not respond. I don't mean to sound pessimistic, but you need to prepare yourself for that possibility."

"I suppose there's not much choice except to at

least try the radiation therapy. How soon will you start? And how long after the treatment will you know if it's successful?"

"According to her medical records, the tumor developed rather rapidly. I'd like to start the therapy immediately, within the week."

The next few weeks were especially stressful for Amanda. She was with her mother for each of her radiation treatments. It was heartbreaking to see her struggling to understand the reason for her physical discomfort.

Amanda's only bright spot was that her presence seemed to comfort her mother. She smiled whenever Amanda entered the room and clung to her hand until it was time for her to leave.

In the back of Amanda's mind was the doctor's caution that the radiation may not be entirely successful. Her mother had had two treatments when Amanda had another interview with the doctor.

He sat across from her, an open folder on the desk. "I'm afraid I have some bad news, Mrs. Connors. The radiation has had very little effect on the tumor. We've also discovered another tumor, and the cancer has spread to her spine."

"There's no other treatment?"

"Under the circumstances, there's nothing I would recommend."

"How long are we talking about, Dr. Aikens?"

"I don't like to give time limits. We can't really say, not with any degree of accuracy. I wouldn't think more than a few months, though."

He closed the folder. "I'm sorry. There's nothing more we can do. I was afraid the fact that the cancer developed so quickly was an indication we might not have much success."

When she left the doctor's office, Amanda returned to the nursing home. After the second treatment, her mother had been transferred back to the only home she had known for years. Amanda spent the rest of the afternoon visiting with her in her room. She tried to come to grips with the fact that she would soon lose her, for the second time.

Amanda had authorized the radiation treatment in hopes that it would provide a miracle. In the back of her mind was Dr. Aikens's caution against pinning her hopes on the treatment.

Amanda watched the sweet, gentle face now. At least her mother would not be subjected to any further illness from the radiation. Amanda had tried to explain the reason for the terrible illness she had suffered. Her mother's blank expression had told her she was having no success.

Elizabeth was not in pain; that was a blessing. Dr. Aikens had explained that the cancer's ultimate destruction of the nervous system would dull the pain. That same destruction would make it necessary for her mother to be hospitalized before long.

When the nurse brought her mother's lunch, she asked Amanda to wait in the lobby until her mother finished her meal. Amanda was pleased to see Mrs. Reed in the lobby. The older woman suggested they go out for lunch rather than sit around in the lobby. Amanda had not planned to tell her about her mother's illness, but the older woman had a gift for drawing information from a person, and Amanda told her the whole story.

"I'm sorry to hear that, Amanda."

"I guess I had been hoping for a miracle with the radiation therapy. The doctor told me it had very little effect on the tumor. Not only that, the cancer is spreading. I'm almost sorry I let them put her through that additional discomfort."

"Amanda, it was a very difficult decision. Even more so, under the circumstances."

"That's the other thing that's been bothering me. Some people would think it doesn't make a lot of difference what happens, considering she hasn't had much of a life for years. Even if there was no cancer, the doctors don't have much hope for her mental state to change.

"Whenever I hear people debating the merits of prolonging life, putting emphasis on the quality of life, I wonder if they've ever been in that position with a loved one. I just keep telling myself that as long as she's alive, one day she might look at me and know who I am."

Evelyn placed her hand over Amanda's. "You can't blame yourself for any of your mother's suffering. You did the best you could. All you can do now is pray. Ultimately, whatever we do or don't do, the outcome is always in God's hands."

"I know, and I have been praying. Even before the tumor was discovered, I prayed for Him to heal her and I've prayed for acceptance if it's not meant for her to be healed. I guess that's really all I can do."

Knowing that her time with her mother was limited, Amanda increased her visits to her mother to include Saturdays. On the other days, she stayed past her usual time. Several times, Drew arrived home before she did. Since she had not yet told him about her mother, she gave him the excuse of shopping or visiting with Nicole.

Less than five weeks after Amanda learned of her mother's illness, she was preparing for her regular Thursday visit when she received a call from Mrs. Lindhurst. Her mother had been admitted to the hospital.

Starting that day, all of Amanda's days off from work were spent at the hospital, including Saturdays and Sundays. She felt guilty when she gave Drew the excuse that she was spending extra time at the shelter or visiting Maya.

Drew did not buy her excuses, but she appeared to be under such stress that he was reluctant to confront her. He continued to hope she would confide in him of her own accord. He stifled the suspicions that nagged at the back of his mind. He could not believe she could be having an affair and continue to exhibit the sweet passion they still shared.

Sixteen

Two weeks after Elizabeth's admission to the hospital, she slipped into a coma. For two days, Amanda sat at her bedside. She had called Mrs. Morris at the shelter on Thursday and explained that she would not be in the next day due to an emergency.

On Saturday evening, Amanda sat patiently at her mother's bedside. She had been there since early morning. A steady rain had been falling all day; it seemed an appropriate setting for her vigil. Amanda paid no attention to the nurses who entered periodically to check the various machines.

She gently stroked her mother's hand, willing her to open her eyes one more time. Her prayer was answered. Elizabeth opened her eyes and looked at her daughter.

"Amanda, it's you. My sweet little baby girl."

Amanda took a deep breath. "Mama? You remember me?"

Elizabeth's breathing became labored. "Of course I remember my baby. You're so beautiful," she rasped.

Amanda could hold the tears back no longer. "Oh, Mama, I've missed you so much."

"I'm so sorry, baby. I love you." She closed her eyes again.

"I love you, too, Mama," Amanda whispered.

Seconds later, the sound of the machine signaled Elizabeth's passing. Amanda did not move. She continued stroking the soft, warm hand. The nurse entered and began disconnecting the machines. Amanda looked up at her questioningly.

"Stay as long as you like, dear. I'll be out of your way in a moment."

Amanda was unaware of the passage of time. She sat holding her mother's hand long after the nurse had left the room. Finally, she roused herself. She rose from the chair, picked up her purse, and left the room. Her mother was no longer there. She was gone to a different place, a better place. Amanda had to hold on to that thought.

Knowing her mother was at peace did not stop the tears. She walked through the chilling rain to her car, her tears mingling with the raindrops that ran down her cheeks.

Drew was worried. It was after eight-thirty in the evening and Amanda had been gone since that morning. Her erratic behavior had worsened in the past two weeks. In addition to that, he had noticed the circles under her eyes. She tried to hide them, but even if she had succeeded, she could not hide the fact that she was not sleeping well. He had been awakened more than once when she left the bed in the middle of the night. It had taken a great deal of restraint not to confront her during one of those restless nights.

The day before, he had finally decided he could wait no longer to learn the truth. He planned to confront her this weekend and insist on some answers. He had to know the reason for her strange behavior, even if his worst fears were confirmed. He had no idea what he would do if she confessed to having an affair. All he knew for sure was that he did not want to lose her.

It had taken every ounce of his self-control not to push for an explanation that morning when she told him she was going to the shelter and then to visit Maya. He hated himself for doing it, but he called the shelter that afternoon. He was not surprised when he was told that she was not there, that she had not been there at all that day.

As dusk settled in, his feelings changed from concern that she was with another man to apprehension for her safety. She had never been out this late without calling.

He was sitting in the den, staring at the telephone and wondering who to call, when he heard the outside garage door open. He reached the door that led from the garage to the kitchen just as she entered. She was drenched from the rain, but that was not the worst detail of her appearance. She looked up at him when he clasped her shoulders.

"Amanda, are you alright? Did you have an accident?"

There was no immediate response. She stared at him blankly. He shook her gently.

"Are you alright? What happened? Where have you been?"

"She's dead," she murmured, her voice barely audible.

Drew's heart pounded. He forced himself to remain calm. He took a deep breath.

"Who's dead, Amanda?"

Amanda forced the words past the lump in her throat. "My mother. She's dead."

Drew was really worried now. What she was saying made no sense.

"Amanda, your mother's been dead for more than eighteen years."

She shook her head. "No, she wasn't. He lied."

She broke down then, murmuring through her sobs. "It's not fair. I finally found her and now I've lost her again. All these years and I never knew."

She shivered. Drew could not be sure if it was from the emotions or if she had caught a chill in the rain. Placing his arm around her shoulders, he urged her from the room and toward the stairs.

Continuing to the bathroom, he stripped her sodden clothes from her body. After drying her off, he helped her into a thick terry cloth robe. Her sobs had quieted, but she could not seem to stop the tears. Lifting her in his arms, he returned to the bedroom and sat down on the sofa with her on his lap.

He sat there holding her, trying to make sense of her words. He could not imagine her anguish. To have believed her mother dead for so long and then learn the truth. How had she learned that her mother was still alive? And what had happened since then? The reasons for the subterfuge had to be connected with her reunion with her mother. But why had she kept it hidden from him?

As he sat there holding his grieving wife, his anger toward her father was rekindled. How could a father do that to his child? To let her believe her mother had died so many years ago? Had he kidnapped her away from her mother after a bitter divorce?

The questions and speculations ricocheted through his mind. He finally let go of the useless conjectures. Amanda would explain it all in good time. For now, it was enough that she was safe in his arms. How could he ever have entertained the idea that she was having an affair?

Drew had hoped to have the answers to his questions

revealed that night, but when he heard her soft, even breathing, he knew any revelations would have to wait until morning. She had exhausted herself.

She did not awaken when he carried her to bed. She only stirred slightly when he eased the robe from her body and tucked her in bed.

Amanda awakened the next morning with a throbbing headache. She sat up gingerly and reached for the robe lying at the foot of the bed. She had just put her arms through the sleeves when Drew entered, carrying a tray.

He set the tray on the bench and sat down on the bed beside her. Brushing her hair back from her face, he lifted her chin and planted a brief, tender kiss on her lips.

"How are you feeling?"

"My head hurts. I was on my way to get something for it."

"I'll get it," he insisted, rising from the bed.

A moment later, he returned with a bottle of pills and a glass of water. She downed two of the tablets and set the glass on the table.

"You should eat something," he suggested. He retrieved the tray from the bench at the foot of the bed and carried it to the sitting area.

She followed him. "I'm not really hungry, Drew. I'll have some coffee, though, please."

She sat down on the sofa and he poured coffee for both of them. He offered her a slice of buttered toast. Seeing the concern in his eyes, she accepted it.

Drew waited patiently for her to finish the toast. He was sure he would now get to the bottom of her strange behavior in the past weeks. The little she had revealed already gave him an idea of what she had been through.

"I'm sorry I worried you, Drew. I should have told you before."

He put his arm around her shoulder. Taking her hand in his, he urged, "Tell me now."

She began her explanation with the discovery of the letter to her father from Dr. Ormond. When she reached the part about her mother's most recent illness, he squeezed her shoulders. She leaned into him and continued, ending with her vigil the previous night.

"You know what's really strange? All the time I've been visiting her, she never recognized me. She didn't even remember having a daughter."

Amanda wiped away a stray tear. "Last night she called me by my name, but not just as someone who's been visiting her. She knew me. She called me her baby girl. She said she loved me."

The tears began to flow more freely. Drew lifted her onto his lap. He felt helpless. What little comfort he could offer could never erase the pain.

When the tears subsided, he asked, "Why didn't you tell me, sweetheart? You shouldn't have carried this alone."

Amanda had known from the beginning that eventually, she would have to explain. "I couldn't bring myself to tell you before. You already know what my father is like. I couldn't tell you that my mother was in a mental hospital."

She tried to pull away from him, but he tightened his hold. "I don't understand that, Amanda."

"You really got a bargain when you married me, didn't you? It was bad enough that my father tried to blackmail you. I couldn't bring myself to tell that my mother's been severely mentally ill for almost twenty years.

"I know, in this day and age, society is supposedly more tolerant of mental illness, but it doesn't always work that way. I guess I just didn't want to give your family more reasons to believe you made a lousy choice for a wife."

Drew lifted her chin, forcing her to look him in the eye. "If you weren't so upset and not thinking straight, I'd be insulted. In answer to your question, yes, I got quite a bargain when I married you. I got an intelligent, beautiful, kind woman whom I happen to love with all my heart and who loves me."

He demonstrated those feelings by kissing her. "As for my family's feelings, I thought we had already settled that. You married me. Whatever my family, or your father, think about us or our marriage has nothing to do with us. It's their problem."

Taking a tissue from the box on the table, he wiped her tear-streaked face. "I have a confession to make, too, Amanda. I knew there was something wrong, that you've been hiding some secret. You've obviously been worried. I would never have guessed the truth. I thought you were having an affair."

Amanda's eyes widened in disbelief. She shook her head. She reached up and touched his cheek, her thumb caressing his lips.

"Oh, sweetheart, I'm so sorry. How could you ever think that? How could I ever want another man? I love you so much."

He placed his hand over hers. Turning his head slightly, he kissed the palm of her hand. He turned his gaze on her face once again.

"No more shouldering problems alone, right?"

Amanda nodded. "Right."

She pulled away from him again. This time, he let her go. She moved from his lap to sit beside him.

After refilling her coffee mug, she continued, "This particular problem is not finished, yet, Drew. I have to make arrangements. I told the hospital I'd be in touch with them. There's no need for an elaborate service, but I don't think my mother had any insurance."

"Amanda, you're not to worry about that. We'll do whatever is necessary, whatever you decide."

Monday morning, Amanda and Drew went together to make the arrangements. Afterward, Drew called the hospital. Later that day, it occurred to Amanda that the nursing home should be informed. She realized the hospital had probably notified them, but she wanted to be certain.

She spoke with Mrs. Lindhurst, who offered her condolences. She informed Amanda that there were a few of her mother's personal possessions still at the nursing home.

"If you like, I can have them packed for you. That will give you a little time to come and get them."

"Thank you, Mrs. Lindhurst. I don't know what the procedure is, but if you know anyone who can use the clothes, feel free to dispose of them."

"That's very kind of you, Mrs. Connors. I'm sure some of our other patients can make use of most of them. The rest we can donate to charity."

"I'll come by for the other items in a week or so, if that's alright."

"That'll be fine."

When she hung up the telephone, Drew raised a question that had been on his mind all day. "Amanda, did you call your father?"

She had not spoken with her father since discovering the letter from Dr. Ormond. At first, she had been too busy trying to locate her mother. Later, she spent all of her free time with her mother. She had no time to concern herself with the person responsible for separating her from her mother.

Aside from those facts, her anger was so great that she had not trusted herself to speak with him. Knowing him as she did, she was sure he would have some excuse for his actions. She also knew that no excuse would satisfy her.

"No, I didn't."

"Would you like for me to do it?"

"Not especially," she said tonelessly. "As far as he's concerned, she died almost twenty years ago. I can't imagine that this news would mean anything to him, or make any difference."

Drew did not press the issue. She had enough on her mind and he could certainly understand her attitude.

The next day, Drew paid a visit to his parents. Amanda had called Nicole and he had contacted Jennifer, but he felt a personal visit to his parents was in order.

"Jennifer called us last night," his father informed him. "I'm confused, though. I understood that Amanda's mother had died when she was a child."

Drew told them the whole story. He watched them closely, his mother in particular, to gauge their reaction to this revelation. He was relieved that their response was more shock than any other emotion.

His father shook his head. "How could a man do that to his child? All those years of believing her mother had died. I can understand not telling a child such distressing news, but once she became an adult. . . . There's no excuse for that."

His mother spoke up then. "You mean Amanda's been carrying this secret around for months?"

"That's right."

"But, why?"

"It's interesting that you should ask that question. She had the idea that we would think less of her if we knew the truth about her mother."

"I can't imagine she would believe that of you," his father said. He sighed. "I wish I could say the same for the rest of this family."

His mother said nothing in her own defense. Although she would never hold her mother's illness against Amanda, her own actions had given her daughter-in-law sufficient reason to expect the worse.

Drew left shortly after delivering his news. He thought he had actually detected some feelings of guilt in his mother's expression. That had not been his intention, but he was not sorry. He had only wanted to assure himself that Amanda's fear of censure was unfounded.

Thursday morning, as Amanda prepared for her mother's funeral, Drew watched her closely. She had held up well through the process of making the necessary arrangements and tying up the loose ends. In spite of that, he was not fooled by her calm facade.

Amanda had not felt comfortable with the idea of having a long church service. Reverend Walters had agreed to conduct the service, but it would be held in the chapel at the cemetery. She was surprised at the people assembled in the small sanctuary when she and Drew arrived.

Nicole and her parents approached as she entered, offering hugs and words of comfort. Mrs. Lindhurst and Dr. Ormond were also present. It made her feel

good that they had taken time out of their busy sched-
ules to pay their last respects to her mother.

As Drew ushered her to her seat, she noticed Mrs.
Reed. Although she and the older woman had become close during their visits to the nursing home,
she never expected her to travel this distance for the
funeral of a virtual stranger. But then, funerals were
not really for the dead, but for the living.

Most surprising of all were Drew's parents—both
of them. She had expected that Drew would tell them
about her mother. She steeled herself for the worst,
but their only reaction was concern and sympathy.
His mother seemed especially subdued. Amanda
briefly wondered about that, but she was in no mood
to question the apparent change in Claire's attitude.

The service was brief. Reverend Walters's final
words brought some comfort to Amanda.

"I never met Elizabeth Reynolds, but I've known her
daughter since she was a child. They say that the first
six years of a person's life are the most important in
determining their character and personality.

"If that's true, Elizabeth must have been a loving
and supportive parent. Her daughter is one of the
kindest, most generous young women I know. She
also has a strength and resilience that is sure to see
her through this difficult time."

Amanda considered Reverend Walters's words and
mentally added to them. She might be strong and
resilient, but she also had good friends, and a loving
husband to help her cope with her grief. She glanced
up at Drew, who had not let go of her hand since
they had entered the chapel. No one could be more
supportive than he had been.

Evelyn noted the conspicuous absence of James
Reynolds. She also noted Drew's loving care and concern for his wife. For what possible reason would

Amanda have hesitated to confide in him? Whatever doubts Amanda may have had concerning her husband's support, it no longer mattered.

She listened to the minister and watched Amanda. Elizabeth would have been proud of her. She also would have been contented to know that her daughter had a husband as loving and supportive as Drew. The young man had not left his wife's side since they had arrived.

When the ceremony had ended and her mother had been laid to rest, a strange calm and peace filled Amanda. She and Drew stood near the car, receiving final condolences. Drew's parents had hung back until most of the others had spoken to the couple.

When his mother approached her, Amanda was wary. The older woman took her hand. The expression on her face showed none of the old animosity.

"I'm very sorry, Amanda. I can only imagine what you've been through." She hesitated, as if she wanted to say more, but simply squeezed her hand and moved away.

Amanda had no opportunity to ponder her mother-in-law's odd behavior. Mrs. Reed approached, but she instinctively deemed a handshake too impersonal. She wrapped her arms around the young woman, kissing her cheek.

"Thank you for coming, Mrs. Reed."

She turned to Drew and introduced him to the older woman. They shook hands as Amanda explained.

"We met at the nursing home. She was visiting a friend."

"Mrs. Lindhurst told me about the service. I wanted to be here for you."

"It's good to see you again, even under these circumstances. I'm going to miss you, and our talks."

"I'll miss you, too, dear."

Drew had been watching the two women. He sensed there was a special bond between them, in spite of their short acquaintance.

"I hope I'm not out of line, but I have a suggestion. I don't see any reason for you not to continue seeing each other. You're welcome to visit us anytime, Mrs. Reed."

Amanda smiled for the first time in weeks. "That sounds like a wonderful idea. Maybe we could even meet for lunch sometimes."

"As a matter of fact, I intend to take Amanda to get something to eat now. She hasn't eaten a decent meal in weeks. Would you care to join us?"

"Thank you, but I'm afraid I have another commitment this afternoon. I would like very much for us to keep in touch, though."

The two women exchanged telephone numbers. Evelyn said her good-byes and Amanda watched as she walked to her car. She could not explain the attachment that had grown between them, but she was glad it would continue.

Seventeen

The week after the funeral, Amanda visited the nursing home one last time to retrieve her mother's personal possessions. She had called Mrs. Reed the day before, suggesting they meet for lunch. They decided to meet at one of the restaurants where they had shared lunch during her mother's illness.

"How are you getting along, Amanda?"

Amanda nodded slowly. "Alright. I returned to work yesterday. That helps a lot. How about you? Has there been any change in your friend?"

Evelyn hesitated. She was still not prepared to tell her young friend the truth.

"Nothing that was unexpected," she replied vaguely.

Amanda sensed she was reluctant to discuss what was probably a hopeless situation. She had been in that situation herself. She refrained from any further questions. For the remainder of the meal, there was no mention of the nursing home.

When she reached home, Amanda carried the boxes containing her mother's possessions upstairs to one of the empty bedrooms. She looked at them for a moment before deciding she was not prepared to examine the contents. It was too soon.

Slowly, her life returned to its normal routine, although she was not quite herself yet. She visited Maya, had lunch with Nicole and even attended a birthday party for David. That occasion reminded her that Drew's birthday was coming up soon.

The two of them were standing in a small alcove, slightly apart from the crowd of guests. "I think this was a great idea. Would you like a party for your birthday?"

Drew looked her up and down. She was wearing a red silk long-sleeved sheath dress that ended just above her knees. He grinned, recalling the matching underwear he had glimpsed earlier that evening when he performed the duty of zipping it up. He shook his head.

"I don't think so. I had something more private in mind."

Amanda rolled her eyes in mock disgust. "I think you have a one-track mind. That might not be a bad idea, though. It'll save me some money and the aggravation of shopping."

Drew laughed. He had missed her sense of humor in the past weeks. He hugged her. "Welcome back, darling. I've missed you."

Amanda's brow wrinkled in confusion. A moment later, his meaning became clear. "I guess until now, I didn't realize I wasn't quite here. It's good to be back. Has it been so terrible for you?"

"No, baby. I've just been concerned about you. I was worried it might take a long time for you to really bounce back."

"You've been very patient with me."

"That's what husbands are for, remember?"

She put her arms around his waist, leaning into

him. She gazed into his eyes, smiling. "Is that all husbands are for?"

Drew's fingers traced a path down her neck and across her collarbone. "You're playing with fire, sweetheart, and when we get home I'll expect you to put it out."

Amanda grinned. "Hmmm, I'm not sure I can live up to those expectations."

His arms came around her waist as he kissed her tenderly, his tongue teasing the corners of her mouth. Amanda's hands clasped his shoulders. All too soon, he broke the kiss.

"Oh, I have no doubt you can live up to my expectations, and beyond."

He sighed. "But for now, I think we could both use a nice cold drink."

"I think you're right. You won't forget where we left off, will you?"

He shook his head. "Not a chance. It won't matter if I do, though. I'll enjoy starting all over from the beginning."

The next morning, Amanda awakened in Drew's arms, his hands lazily caressing her silky skin. Amanda murmured sleepily, "What's the verdict? Did I live up to your expectations?"

Drew chuckled. "As a matter of fact, I think you might have to try it again."

Amanda playfully pinched his thigh before smoothing over the spot lightly with her fingers. Drew groaned when her hand traveled higher and began to tease the mat of hair surrounding the shaft of his manhood. His arousal was almost immediate and soon their bodies were joined in passion once again.

After the passion was spent, it was more than a few

minutes before either of them stirred again. Drew was the first to speak.

"It's times like this when a robot would come in handy. To be able to just press a button and have a machine bring our breakfast would be wonderful."

Amanda smiled. "I think a machine is a great idea. It would never do to have a live-in maid, considering your propensity for making love at the drop of a hat, wherever we might be at the time."

"Is that a complaint?"

She snuggled closer. "What do you think?"

His hands continued stroking her soft skin. "Judging from the moans and whimpers I heard a little while ago, I think not." He sighed. "Unfortunately, this is not getting our breakfast made. Shall we toss a coin?"

"There's no point in doing that. It won't matter if I win. It's no fun in bed alone."

She extricated herself from his embrace. After sliding across the bed, she stood up and headed for the bathroom. Drew called after her.

"I don't suppose you'd like to share your shower."

She looked over her shoulder, grinning. "If you do, I think we'll be more concerned with lunch than breakfast."

The week after David's birthday, Amanda was offered a full-time position with one of the mental health centers. The decision to change jobs was not as difficult as leaving her former job when she and Drew reconciled. Because her patients at the shelter were in transition, she had not developed the attachments she had with her previous patients.

A week into her new job, she met a young patient who struck a personal chord. She reminded Amanda of the verbal and emotional abuse she herself had suffered. In this case, the child's mother was the source of the abuse and there was no one to counteract its effects. After the first few sessions, Amanda felt her anger against her own father being stirred up again.

The Saturday after the first week of her new job, she had lunch with Mrs. Reed. She shared the news of her new job.

"That's wonderful, Amanda. I'm happy for you."

Amanda pushed the food around on her plate. "One of my patients stirred up some feelings I thought I had overcome."

"What kinds of feelings?"

"Anger. You wouldn't know it, but my father wasn't at the funeral. I refused to contact him, not that I think it would have made a difference. The fact is, I haven't spoken to him since I found the letter from Dr. Ormond. I didn't trust myself to confront him with that discovery."

"And now you plan to confront him. If your anger has been stirred up again, how can you trust yourself to confront him now?"

Amanda sighed. "I know what you're saying, but I also know that I won't be satisfied until I do. I'll just have to work on subduing the anger before I follow through with it."

Amanda's idea about confronting her father was set aside with the approach of Drew's birthday. His birthday fell on a Thursday, but she let it go with no notice. She could tell by his attitude that he was disappointed, but he made no mention of her oversight.

The evening following Drew's birthday, when he arrived home, the aroma of pot roast greeted him.

Amanda entered the kitchen just as he was inspecting the contents of the oven.

She stood in the doorway a moment, watching him, before calling attention to herself. She cleared her throat.

Drew closed the oven door and turned to face her. She was wearing a sheer, black lace-trimmed peignoir set.

She walked over to him, took his face in her hands, and kissed him. Drew's arms automatically encircled her, drawing her closer as he deepened the kiss.

After a while, Amanda broke the kiss. "Happy birthday."

He opened his mouth, but she placed her finger on his lips, forestalling his reply. "Yes, I know it was yesterday, but I thought the celebration should be saved for today since you don't have to go to the office tomorrow."

Drew grinned. "I'm not sure if you're saying that to cover the fact that you forgot. If that's the case"— he stepped back and looked her up and down—"I'm more than willing to ignore that oversight."

Amanda took a step back. "Dinner is almost ready. Why don't you get out of that suit and tie while I put it on the table?"

Drew returned a short time later as Amanda placed the final dish on the table in the breakfast area. She glanced over at him.

"I decided this was cozier than that big dining room table."

She lit the candles and they sat down to eat. Drew was in the process of carving the roast when she spoke again.

"I had a hard time deciding what to wear for dinner. I considered wearing a bib apron."

Drew's attention was focused on the dangerous instrument in his hand. "I think it would have been a wise move, working at the stove. That outfit is probably highly flammable."

"I didn't cook in this. I put it on after everything else was done and the roast was in the oven."

Amanda placed her elbows on the table and linked her hands beneath her chin. Grinning, she watched him closely.

"I think you missed the point, though. I was going to wear a bib apron, period."

Drew looked up from his task. "You realize that comment almost cost me a finger?"

Amanda laughed. "Sorry, sweetheart. No more innuendoes until after the carving, I promise."

After dinner, Drew insisted on helping with the cleanup. "We can finish much faster together."

"What's your hurry? I told you I planned this tonight so there would be no rush."

"The rush is getting to the good part of the evening."

"Are you insinuating that dinner wasn't good?"

He came up behind her, put his arms around her, and nuzzled her neck. "Dinner was delicious, but that's only one appetite. Sitting across from you in that outfit has increased my other appetite considerably."

As expected, a short time later, they started up the stairs. When they reached the bedroom, Amanda turned to face Drew. After shedding her robe, she began unbuttoning his shirt.

"What you need is a nice relaxing massage."

She removed every article of his clothing and spread a towel on the bed. She then instructed him to lie down on his stomach.

Slowly, she began massaging the oil into the muscles of his shoulders and arms. Her breasts grazed his spine when she leaned over to reach the arm on the far side of his torso. Amanda took a deep breath to restore her composure. She had a long way to go before the massage was finished.

Her hands moved to his torso and she began working the oil into the muscles of his back and down his body to the taut muscles of his buttocks. They lingered there, gently kneading, before moving down and between his thighs.

Drew groaned. "Is this supposed to be pleasure or torture?"

"What's that saying, 'no pain, no gain?'

"I don't think that was meant to apply to this situation."

Amanda chuckled. Her hands stilled. "In that case, maybe I should stop."

"That, sweetheart, would really be torture."

Amanda's fingers continued their journey down his legs. When she had finished, she instructed him to turn over on his back.

The sight of his arousal was almost her undoing. Drew noticed the look on her face and grinned. He laid back against the pillows with his hands beneath his head, totally relaxed.

She smoothed the oil across his collarbone and down his chest to his abdomen. Trying very hard to ignore his arousal, she worked the oil into the fronts of his thighs and down his legs.

"You missed a spot," he informed her.

Amanda knew he was not referring to any area of his torso or legs. If there had been any doubt in her mind, he made his meaning clear when he reached over and took her hand. She swallowed hard when he placed it on his lower abdomen.

Their gazes locked. Drew reached up and eased

the strap of her gown over her shoulder. He tugged
the other strap down, exposing most of both full,
round breasts.

Amanda's hand moved a few inches lower to play
in the mat of hair surrounding his now fully aroused
shaft. Drew held his breath when she ran the tip of
her finger down the length of the shaft itself.

He removed his other hand from beneath his head
and sat up. He pulled her across his lap to lie beside
him.

"I think the massage is finished," he murmured,
a second before his mouth came down on hers.

He quickly disposed of her gown and began his
own explorations. When his hands caressed the curls
at the juncture of her thighs, it was Amanda's turn
to groan. His fingers moved even lower, stroking the
sensitive nub. Her body jerked in response.

"Please, Drew, I need you now."

He eased his body between her soft thighs. When
he entered her in one long stroke, they sighed in
unison. As the pace of his thrusts increased, the tension built until Amanda felt as if she would explode.

"Oh, baby, you feel so good," Drew whispered.

Seconds later, the flames of passion erupted. They
clung to each other as the waves of pleasure washed
over them, finally reducing the fire to warm, glowing
embers. Sated, they drifted off to sleep.

After Drew's birthday, Amanda's attention again
became focused on her determination to have it out
with her father. Maybe he had a good reason for not
telling her about her mother. The least she could do
was give him an opportunity to explain.

Once again, she kept her plans from Drew. She
told herself that this situation was not the same as

with her mother's illness. This matter was between her and her father.

Drew was conducting another seminar that week, so she chose Thursday evening for her visit. She had no idea what hours her father worked, but she took a chance on driving directly to see him when she left work.

There had been no improvements in the house. In fact, the postage stamp-sized lawn looked as if it would soon be totally overrun with weeds. She surveyed the area with its modest row homes. She could imagine the other residents on the block were not too pleased with the state of their neighbor's lawn. She sighed and walked to the front door.

After knocking several times, the door was finally opened. Her father did not look as if he had just come from work. He was unshaven and his eyes were red. Surprisingly, he stood aside to allow her to enter.

"What are you doing here? Did you come to gloat, to lord it over me?" He sneered, ambling back to the living room. Amanda followed him, noting that he limped slightly.

"No, I didn't come to gloat. How's your leg?"

"My leg's fine." He turned around to face her.

"Has the doctor released you to return to work?"

The sound he emitted was more of a snort than a laugh. "Yeah, he released me. So did the job. Said they couldn't hold it until I was ready to come back."

"You mean you've been out of work all this time?"

"Yeah, why?"

"I just wondered how you've been managing."

"You planning to make a contribution?" Amanda came close to doing just that. Then she remembered the reason for her visit.

"That's not why I'm here. I came to tell you Mom's dead, really dead."

He swung around to face her. "How did you find out?"

"Does it matter? Why, Dad? Why did you let me think she was dead all these years?"

James thought fast. For a brief moment, he had seen the sympathy in her eyes when he told her about the job. If he told her the truth, she would have nothing else to do with him.

"You were only seven years old. I couldn't tell you that your mother was in a mental hospital. The doctor said there wasn't much hope. What else could I do?"

He held his breath, waiting for her response. His story sounded good to him.

"You could have told me later."

He shrugged, trying to look contrite. "I didn't know how."

"Why didn't you go to see her?"

He paused, thinking. "I did at first, but I couldn't stand seeing her like that."

James cleared his throat. His next words did not come easy for him. "I'm sorry. I did the best I could."

Amanda recalled her reaction the first time she saw her mother. She had known for years that her father was a weak person. Did she have the right to hold that against him? She had vowed to give him the benefit of the doubt. Maybe it was really time to let it go.

She reached in her purse and pulled out her wallet. "Do you need some money to tide you over?"

He hesitated, stifling the feeling of victory. "I don't want any charity from you."

"It's not charity. You're my father."

Amanda gave him all the cash she had in her wallet. She could stop at the ATM on her way home.

The fact that she did not write a check did not escape his notice. Obviously, she preferred not to have her husband know what she was doing.

As she drove home, Amanda felt a twinge of guilt. Part of her guilt was due to the possibility that she may have misjudged her father. The other part was her failure to confide in Drew. She assuaged her guilt concerning Drew with the conviction that he would never understand her offer of help to her father. There was no need to cause a disagreement over such a trivial matter. It was not as if she had given him thousands, or even hundreds, of dollars.

On Saturday, Amanda had lunch with Mrs. Reed again. The older woman had become quite a confidante to Amanda as a result of the circumstances of their first meeting. She told her about the visit with her father.

"I can understand his difficulty with seeing my mother in her mental condition."

Evelyn bit back her instinctive response to that assessment. She knew James Reynolds well enough to know that compassion had never motivated any of his actions.

"I felt bad for him. I can't believe they wouldn't hold his job for him. I don't know how he's been managing."

Something in her words alerted Evelyn. "Amanda, I suppose it's none of my business and if so, just say so. You didn't give him money, did you?"

She shrugged. "Just a few dollars. It's not like he asked me for it. In fact, he was reluctant to take it. How could I not help him? Even if it means giving him more money, I can't let him lose the house, if there's something I can do to help."

"Is it the same house where you lived as a child?"

Amanda nodded. In her mind's eye, she saw an image of the way the house looked when she lived there. Then she recalled the picture of its current condition.

"It's a little run-down, but it's a nice neighborhood. Are you familiar with Philadelphia?"

"A little. I have a friend who used to live on a small street near Germantown Avenue years ago. She moved to North Carolina to live with her son, but we still keep in touch."

"I can't believe it! We lived in Germantown, too."

The two women went off on a tangent, discussing the old neighborhood and other interesting areas of Philadelphia. The discussion eventually came back to her childhood home and her father.

"Is he really in such dire straits, Amanda? Doesn't he have any savings? What about unemployment compensation?"

"I didn't ask him about that."

Her tone of voice changed. Evelyn suspected her young friend was becoming irritated by her questions about James. She hoped Amanda would not allow James to take advantage of her. The young woman had such a generous spirit, too generous where her father was concerned.

Before they parted company, Amanda invited Evelyn to dinner the following week. She wrote down the address and directions.

"Drew's been asking about you. Is Sunday, about three o'clock good?"

"That sounds fine. I'll enjoy seeing him again."

Eighteen

On Sunday afternoon when she and Drew returned from church, Amanda began preparing dinner for her guest. Drew had gone upstairs to change clothes. She was placing the ham in the oven when he joined her in the kitchen.

"Anything I can do to help?"

"You can set the table. It's about time we christened our new dining room set."

"Are you going to change into something more comfortable?"

She was still wearing the pale blue linen dress she had worn to church. She looked down at her stockinged feet.

"I guess I should. I wanted to put the ham in first. Stopping at the bakery took more time than I expected."

Mrs. Reed arrived a little after two-thirty. Drew opened the door to their visitor.

"It's good to see you again. Did you have any trouble finding the house?"

"Not at all. Amanda gave me very good directions."

She looked around. "You have a beautiful home."

"Thank you. I'm sure Amanda will want to give you the tour."

At that moment, Amanda joined them. She greeted her friend with a hug. "I'm so glad you came."

She glanced at Drew. "I heard his suggestion. Would you like to see the house?"

"I'd love it."

Amanda led her up the stairs. After showing her the master bedroom, she led her down the hall.

When they reached the third room, she explained, "This is the only other bedroom that's furnished. At the moment, the others are either empty or being used for storage."

"It's a big house to furnish. I imagine it would take some time to complete the job."

"We're in no hurry. The house needed quite a few repairs when Drew bought it. He decided a roof that didn't leak and a decent kitchen were more important than filling the rooms with furniture."

"That's very sensible. I think too many young people get in over their heads, thinking they have to completely furnish a new house immediately."

They proceeded down the stairs and across the hall. Evelyn was as impressed with the piano as Amanda had been. She ran her fingers over the polished wood.

"It's a beautiful instrument, Amanda. Which one of you plays?"

Amanda smiled. "Actually, I just recently started taking lessons again. I took them for about two years before we moved. Drew found this at an auction and couldn't resist it."

Evelyn nodded. Her young friend's wistful expression told her there was more to that story. Whatever the explanation, it obviously was a pleasant memory.

The remainder of the afternoon passed pleasantly.

Amanda had one precarious moment when it occurred to her that her guest might inadvertently mention her visits to her father. She relaxed when she realized there would be no reason for that topic to arise.

The following week, Amanda decided it was time to see what was in the box holding her mother's possessions. The fact that there were so few items in the box was itself heartbreaking.

There were a few pieces of jewelry, a wedding band, an inexpensive watch, and a charm bracelet. Amanda examined the charm bracelet. It held only three charms: a mortarboard, a heart inscribed with "I Love You," and a miniature piano.

The last item brought back memories of sitting beside a woman who was playing the most beautiful, soothing music she had ever heard. It was her mother who had insisted on her taking piano lessons.

As she dug through the box, she came up with a few strange items. There was an exquisitely knit baby blanket and sweater set. They must have been made for the baby who never had a chance to experience life. She fingered the delicate garments tenderly. She wondered, briefly, who had taken the time and attention to wrap them so carefully in tissue paper. Whoever it was, she was grateful to them. One day they would be put to use. Elizabeth's child never had the opportunity to wear them, but her grandchildren would.

Thinking about her mother naturally brought her father to mind. That, in turn, reminded her of Mrs. Reed's questions. His income had probably decreased considerably with the loss of his job as bailiff. That would explain the lack of savings. Amanda knew little about the qualifications for unemployment benefits, but she could think of no reason for him not to collect. If that was the case, he was just using her.

The following Saturday, Amanda paid her father another visit. She rang the bell, but there was no answer. She tried knocking, but there was still no response.

She hated going back home without accomplishing her purpose. She had spent days gearing herself up for this meeting. The questions raised by Mrs. Reed had aroused her curiosity. She needed to get some answers to her questions about his financial situation.

She decided to wait. Maybe he would return soon. Taking a tissue from her purse, she wiped off the old swing on the porch and sat down.

Fifteen minutes passed and her father had not returned. She had risen from the swing, preparing to leave, when the mailman arrived. He greeted her cheerfully and handed her a batch of envelopes. Before she could explain that she did not live there, he was halfway down the stairs. She shrugged and went to slip the bundle through the mail slot.

She reached the door, but before dropping the mail in the opening, her curiosity got the best of her. She was not looking for anything in particular, but she discovered a very interesting piece of mail.

There was an envelope from the Department of Labor and Industry, Bureau of Unemployment Compensation Benefits and Allowances. Amanda knew the envelope was no proof of what she suspected, but it certainly hinted that Mrs. Reed's suggestion was a distinct possibility. She dropped the mail in the slot.

She had turned to leave when her father drove up. He stepped out of the car and started toward the house. He mumbled a greeting, barely looking at her, and unlocked the door. Amanda followed him as he scooped up the mail, leafing through it as he walked to the living room.

"What brings you back here? You got another handout for your dear old dad?" He asked, continuing toward the kitchen.

Amanda waited patiently. She had smelled the alcohol on his breath when he passed her on the porch. The last thing he needed was another beer, but he returned with one in his hand. The anger she had stifled before her last visit rose up even stronger.

"Haven't you found a job, yet?"

"Not a lot of jobs out there for a man my age."

"Have you even looked?"

His eyes narrowed. "What kind of question is that? It sounds like something your rich husband would say. Did he find out you gave me a few bucks?"

"Drew has nothing to do with this. You haven't answered my question."

He was fuming inwardly. Who did she think she was, to question him like he was some kid? He would put up with it for a little longer, though. He knew her. She had a soft heart. She would feel guilty if she thought he was about to be evicted and she did nothing to stop it.

"Sure I looked." He lied, taking a swallow from the can of beer.

"What about unemployment compensation?"

He almost choked on the beer. "What about it? I got fired, remember."

"That's not what you told me. You said they wouldn't hold your job while you recuperated. That's not the same thing."

He turned on her. "What are you trying to say? It's none of your business anyway."

"I'm saying you never stop, do you? You'd take and take until there's nothing left."

Within minutes, their voices were raised in anger. "Is this what you learned from that rich husband of yours, disrespect for your father?"

"I came here to offer help because I thought you were in need. You didn't need my help. You just wanted to see how much you could take from me."

"You're supposed to help me. I'm your father."

"You're awfully free with that title, for someone who did little to earn it. In my profession I've come across some sorry excuses for fathers. You may not be as bad as the worst I've seen, but you certainly come in a close second."

"I guess you got that backbone from that husband, too. Your mother sure never had any."

That was the final straw for Amanda. She picked up the nearest item, which happened to be a lamp. She had every intention of throwing it at him, but his reaction stopped her.

"Yeah, go ahead throw it. You try to act so cool and controlled. You've been itching to do something like that for years."

Amanda set the lamp back down on the table. He was half right. She had wanted to hit him many times when she lived with him. She was a teenager then. She was also wise enough then to know matters would only become worse if she lost control. She thought she had overcome that urge since she had matured. She turned to leave and he laughed.

"I guess underneath you're just like her after all."

The thread of control that had held her back was very fine. Even so, it might have held if he had kept silent just one more minute. His final comment was all it needed to snap.

She picked up the ashtray next to the lamp and hurled it across the room, narrowly missing his head.

Before he could recover from the shock, she was out the door, in her car and driving away.

Amanda did not go directly home. She had to cool off first, to regain her composure. She could not believe she had actually thrown an ashtray at her father! She could not let Drew see her like this. She would be forced to explain the reason for the residual effects of her fury. He would undoubtedly be angry if he knew she had visited her father twice without telling him.

She remembered all the times she had given Drew the excuse of shopping when she was visiting her mother, and returned home empty-handed. She had given him the same excuse that morning. She headed for the mall—this time she would have packages to show for her outing.

While Amanda was shopping, her father was opening the door to another visitor. Evelyn had decided to take matters into her own hands. She knew that as long as Amanda thought her father needed help, she would continue to give it.

She rang the bell and waited. Amanda had to know the truth. She would try to convince James to tell her the truth. If he refused . . . well, she would think about that later.

James opened the door, trying to focus through his alcoholic stupor. He half expected to see Amanda, returning to apologize. He should have known better. She had always been a problem. He had never been able to control her the way he did her mother.

"Who are you? What do you want? Whatever you're selling, I don't want any."

"I'm not selling anything, James. I don't know if you remember me. I'm Evelyn Reed."

There was a glimmer of something in his expression. Not quite recognition, but something. She did not wait for him to invite her in. She opened the storm door and, oddly enough, he stepped back, allowing her to enter.

"We need to talk, you and I, James Reynolds."

Evelyn marched into the living room with him following behind. "We need to talk about Amanda," she repeated.

"What do you mean we need to talk about Amanda? Who are you? What do you know about Amanda?"

"I know everything about Amanda, and I know you've been taking advantage of her good-hearted nature."

As she explained the reason for her visit, recognition dawned. How had this busybody found him? How had she met Amanda? As she talked, his anger grew.

"Get out of my house! I don't have to listen to anything you have to say."

"You're right, you don't have to listen to me. Obviously, you have no intention of telling Amanda the truth, so I'll do it myself."

Although Amanda had been angry when she left, he might be able to bring her around. Unemployment compensation would not last forever. This meddlesome woman could ruin everything.

"Listen, you old busybody. You better stay out of my business. You tried to get between me and Elizabeth, filling her head with a lot of foolishness."

"Amanda's not like her mother; she's strong. She'll see you for what you are when I tell her the truth."

She turned to go and he snatched her from behind. Whirling her around, he grabbed her by the shoulders, shaking her. He continued with his diatribe and threats.

Evelyn had never considered the possibility that he

might be dangerous. The look in his eyes now changed that opinion. She tried to get away from him and stumbled back against the table. Her sudden move and his own alcoholic clumsiness dislodged his hands from her shoulders. When he came at her again, she instinctively picked up the lamp and swung it at him. It caught him squarely on the side of his temple. He was dazed by the blow and the shocking realization that she had actually hit him. Evelyn quickly made her escape as he staggered back and fell to the floor.

When she reached her car, she sat there for a few minutes, looking in the rearview mirror to be sure he was not coming after her. The car doors were locked, but recalling the rage she had seen in his eyes, she could not be sure what he might try to do. With that in mind, she started the car and left.

Nineteen

On Monday evening, Amanda and Drew finished dinner and retired to the den. They had barely entered the room when the telephone rang. Drew answered it while she settled comfortably on the sofa.

"Hello, Drew," Nicole responded to his greeting. "Is Amanda there?"

"Sure, just a minute."

"No, I don't need to speak to her. You'd better turn on the TV, the news."

Drew did as she suggested, flipping to the channel she indicated. Amanda's attention was also now focused on the screen. The reporter was standing outside a modest row home, telling the audience about a discovery that had recently been made inside the house, her father's house.

"Two neighbors were alerted to the possibility that something might be amiss. It seems the neighbors had become fed up with the unsightly condition of Mr. Reynolds's yard and elected an emissary to discuss the situation with him.

"When they approached the front door, it was slightly ajar and they were struck by a strange odor. They immediately called the police, who discovered the body of Mr. Reynolds."

Amanda did not hear the rest of the story. "I can't believe it. It can't be. I just saw him Saturday."

Drew stared at her. "You went to see him?"

Amanda nodded. "Yes, I decided I had to tell him about my mother's death."

"And?"

"And, he couldn't care less."

"Why didn't you tell me? Why the deception about shopping?"

"I did go shopping."

"Like you did all those times you were really visiting your mother?"

"You're not being fair, Drew. I explained why I didn't tell you about that."

"Yes, Amanda, you explained, but you still didn't see fit to confide in me when you decided to visit your father. Did Mrs. Reed know about this visit?"

"Mrs. Reed?"

"Yes, you seem to be able to confide in her, a total stranger, more than you can confide in me."

"It's not the same. She knew about my mother because I met her at the nursing home."

"You're right. It's not the same," he said, running his hand through his hair.

Amanda avoided his gaze. How could she explain that she had not wanted to subject him to her father's animosity? No, she had to be honest with herself. There was more to it than that. She knew he would not approve of her giving her father money. And he would have been right. Had she actually been trying to buy her father's approval after all these years?

There was no more discussion that evening. In fact, there was no conversation at all. Drew left the room shortly after their discussion. Amanda heard the outside garage door open, and then close. She heard him drive off.

* * *

Drew had to get away, get some fresh air and clear his head. He was angry. No, that was not quite true. It was not so much anger as it was pain. He had felt this pain before. He felt it when she left, rather than discuss her problems with their marriage. He felt it again when she neglected to tell him about her mother. Neither time had hurt as much as this, or maybe it was merely a combination of all those times.

Along with the pain was frustration. He thought she would have learned to trust him by now. He was at a loss as to what he could do to assure her. Underneath the pain and frustration, there was fear. He was afraid she would never trust him completely. That brought out the ultimate fear. How could love survive without trust? If she did not learn to trust him, he would eventually lose her.

He drove around for a while and finally ended up at his office. He unlocked the door and let himself into the deserted building. Maybe a little work would help him calm down.

He turned on the light switch and started toward his office. He set to work, blotting out everything else. An hour later, he looked up from the papers and straight into his wife's face in the photograph on his desk. He put the papers aside and stood up. It was time to go home.

He closed the door of his private office and started toward the door. He had only gone a few feet when he stopped. His eyes were focused on the small desk that sat close to his secretary's desk, Amanda's old desk. It was someone else's desk now. In his mind's eye, though, it was Amanda he saw sitting there, busily keying in data from the folders beside her. He remembered how hard she had worked, how eager she was to learn.

He remembered something else, too. In those days he had seldom seen her smile. There was always a hint of pain in her eyes, although she never voiced any discontent.

He thought the pain had been banished after all these years. She probably thought so too, until it had all been resurrected with the discovery that her mother had been alive all this time. To lose her again so soon had to have been devastating. How could he expect her to think clearly?

The fact that she knew how he felt about her father was no help. It was no wonder she had chosen to keep her visit a secret from him. She had hurt him by not trusting him, but she was in pain, too.

The den was empty when Drew reached home. He turned out the lights and headed for bed. The lights were off in the bedroom and, judging from the soft sound of her breathing as he neared the bed, Amanda was asleep. A faint sliver of moonlight fell across her face. Drew stood beside the bed watching her before leaning over and kissing her cheek. It was still moist. She had been crying and it was his fault.

He undressed and slid into bed. She whimpered softly in her sleep when he pulled her into his arms. Holding her close, he kissed her temple and settled back onto the pillows.

"It's alright, baby," he whispered. "Everything will be alright."

* * *

Amanda awakened the next morning still wrapped in Drew's embrace. She stirred and looked up into his face, expecting him to be asleep.

"Good morning," he murmured.

"Morning." Brushing her hair back from her eyes, she tried to extricate herself. Drew loosened his hold and she moved across the bed, stood up and started toward the bathroom. She stopped halfway across the room when he called her name.

"What are you planning to do today?"

"What do you mean?"

"Don't you think you should go and identify yourself to the police? I'm sure they'll be looking for your father's closest relative."

"I guess you're right. That hadn't really occurred to me."

She stood there for a moment, thinking about his suggestion. After their disagreement the previous evening, she had been unable to think about anything else. The idea of going to the police station was upsetting enough in itself. It now occurred to her that she would have to make arrangements for another funeral.

Drew watched as the expression on her face revealed her troubled emotions. He made no further comment. It was her move.

She avoided his gaze. "Drew?"

"Yes," he said expectantly.

She took a deep breath and looked over at him. "Will you come with me?"

Drew threw back the covers, stood up and closed the space between them. She looked up into the ebony eyes that held so much love, in spite of everything. He opened his arms and she stepped into his strong, loving embrace. He placed a warm kiss on her temple, gently stroking her back.

"Of course I'll come with you, Amanda. Do you think I'd let you go through this alone?"

She leaned back and looked up into his eyes. "I'm sorry, Drew. I know I should have told you, but. . . ."

He placed a finger on her lips, stopping her words. "It's alright, sweetheart. None of that's important now. I'm sorry I walked out on you."

He removed his finger and planted a brief kiss on her mouth. "We'll handle this together."

Less than two hours later, they walked into the police station hand in hand. When Amanda explained her reason for coming, she was directed to the officer in charge of the investigation. He ushered them into a small room.

"Mrs. Connors, I understand you're James Reynolds's daughter. First of all, you have my condolences on your loss."

"Thank you. Can you tell me what happened?"

"Well, the truth is, I was hoping you'd be able to shed some light on that matter."

"There's not really anything I can tell you. I wasn't aware of any illness. My father and I haven't had much contact in years."

Sergeant Lafferty hesitated. "Mrs. Connors, how much do you know about your father's death?"

She shrugged. "Only the little I saw on the news on TV. Why?"

"Your father sustained some head injuries. We won't know the specific cause of death until after the autopsy, but it doesn't appear to be from natural causes. His death may have been accidental, but we can't rule out the possibility of homicide."

"Homicide? That doesn't make sense. Who would want to kill my father? And why?"

He shook his head. "As I said, I was hoping that you or his neighbors would be able to give us some ideas about that."

He paused, leafing through the papers in the folder on the table. It contained very little information, but there was one interesting report from the officer who questioned the neighbors.

"You mentioned that you hadn't had much contact with your father. When was the last time you saw him?"

"I went to see him last Saturday."

"What time was that?"

"I think about eleven-fifteen, maybe eleven-thirty."

"Was there any particular reason for your visit?"

Drew had sat quietly listening to the exchange. When the questions took this subtle turn from simply obtaining general information about her father, he decided to put a stop to it.

"Sergeant, this line of questioning seems to indicate the advisability of my wife having an attorney present."

Amanda's eyes widened as she turned to face him. "What are you saying, Drew?"

"I'm saying that I think you should consult an attorney before you answer any more of the sergeant's questions."

She turned back to Sergeant Lafferty. "Is he right? Are you suggesting I had something to do with my father's death?"

"I'm not suggesting anything, at the moment. I'm merely conducting an investigation. Until we get the autopsy report, I have to consider all possibilities."

"I can't believe this. I came here because as far as I know, my father had no other relatives, at least no other close relatives. I'm the one who'll be responsible for making arrangements for the funeral."

"I'm afraid that will have to wait. We can't release the body until after the autopsy."

Amanda stood up. "In that case, I'd appreciate it

if you would let me know when I can begin making arrangements."

"Very well, Mrs. Connors, if that's the way you want it."

Amanda was very quiet on the drive back to the house. If Drew was correct and the police suspected that she was somehow involved in her father's death, they would be even more suspicious if they learned about their argument.

"Amanda?"

"Yes?"

"My suggestion that you speak with an attorney is just a precaution. I can't believe the police seriously think you had anything to do with your father's death."

"Maybe not, but there's something you need to know. We had quite an argument on Saturday."

"It's about time."

She glanced at him. "What do you mean?"

"I mean that considering all you suffered from your father, it's surprising that you haven't lost your temper before now."

"I have you to thank for that. Once you took me out of that situation, it was finished. There was no reason to be angry with him, until I found out about my mother."

Drew reached over and took her hand. "I love you, Amanda. For years, I told myself I married you to save you from him, but I think there's always been more to it than that."

Amanda placed her other hand on top of their clasped hands. "What you felt, or didn't feel, years ago doesn't matter. I'm just glad to have you here with me now."

* * *

Later that afternoon, Drew drove her to an attorney's office. Claude Oglethorpe was an old friend of Drew's family. Drew had called him when they returned from the police station. He explained the situation and the older man arranged to see them that day.

"Okay, Drew, you told me the basics of the circumstances, but what makes you think you need my services? What did the police say?"

"Not much; they asked a few questions. When I saw the direction they were headed, I suggested Amanda not answer any more of their questions."

"Did they read you your rights, Amanda?"

"No, I identified myself and asked for information about what happened to my father. That's when Sergeant Lafferty told me his death was not from natural causes. He suggested it might have been an accident. When he started asking about my visit, Drew stopped him. I guess I wasn't thinking straight. It seemed so ridiculous for him to think I had anything to do it."

"Tell me about your visit."

She told him everything, beginning with finding the letter that led her to her mother. She explained the reason for the visit to her father and the ensuing argument.

"Just before I left, I threw an ashtray at him, but I missed. He was perfectly fine when I left. In fact, he seemed very pleased with himself that he had goaded me into such a reaction."

Claude was thoughtful as he listened to her narrative. He found it hard to believe that this young woman could be guilty of murder, even in the heat of an argument.

"Well, I think the best thing to do is wait and see what the police have in mind. It's very likely they're simply looking for information."

He folded his hands on the desk. "I wouldn't recommend that you answer any further questions unless I'm present."

Amanda nodded. "Do you think there's a chance they'll arrest me?" she asked, her voice barely above a whisper.

"I'll be honest with you. It depends on what they turn up in their investigation. Have they determined when death occurred?"

Drew and Amanda shook their heads. Drew answered. "We have no idea. They're probably waiting for the autopsy to make that determination. At any rate, Sergeant Lafferty didn't tell us."

"I'll see what I can find out. Meanwhile, we'll assume the best. I know it's easier said than done, Amanda, but try not to worry."

Twenty

Somehow, Amanda survived the rest of the week. There was no further word from the police concerning the investigation. She tried to convince herself that no news was good news, but that old adage did not seem to work in this circumstance.

The police had given her permission to enter her father's house, but she felt no immediate need to make another visit to her old home. She had no reason to go there yet. Eventually, she would have to go through his papers to settle his financial affairs, but that could wait a little longer.

On Friday, she received a call informing her that she could claim the body. That evening after dinner while they were in the process of loading the dishwasher, she told Drew that the funeral arrangements could be made.

She closed the dishwasher and walked back toward the table. She looked so tired. He took her by the hand and urged her out of the kitchen, through the living room and into the den. She settled on the sofa and he sat down beside her, taking both her hands in his.

"What do you want to do, Amanda?"

"I don't know, Drew. Do we have to have a funeral?"

"We don't have to do anything you don't want to

do. You don't have to decide tonight. Why don't we
let it wait until morning?"

She nodded. "I'll have to go back to the house. I
don't even know if he had insurance."

"We'll worry about that later," he insisted, his arms
encircling her.

He pulled her onto his lap and settled back against
the cushions. Amanda sighed and leaned into his embrace. After a while, the tension in her body eased.
They were both content to simply have a quiet moment together. The time since she located her mother
had been so nerve-racking for Amanda that most of
their time together had been filled with tension.

The following Wednesday, there was a short service
at the funeral home. A few of the neighbors attended
the brief service and offered their condolences. They
were the reason Amanda had decided to have a service
at all. Several of them had inquired about her plans
when she was at the house the previous Saturday.

When she started making the plans, Amanda had
insisted on a separate cemetery plot for her father.
Although Drew had made no comment on that decision, she felt the need to explain. After the way he
had treated her mother, she could not bring herself
to put them in the same plot or even near each other.

"I guess that sounds really strange. After all, their
spirits are somewhere else, so what difference could
it make where their bodies are placed?"

"I guess it doesn't really matter except that if it
makes you feel better, that's all that counts, sweetheart."

Reluctantly, Amanda had taken leave from her job
for the week of her father's funeral. She spent the

remaining days trying to organize her father's financial affairs. She had heard no more about the police investigation and she was trying to take the attorney's advice not to worry.

On Thursday afternoon, that advice went up the chimney. Drew arrived home early, accompanied by Claude. He had obtained more information on his own.

"I sent one of my investigators to talk to the neighbors. He learned that your father's next-door neighbor overheard your argument. What time did you leave there?"

"I wasn't there long. I guess it must have been about noon. Why?"

"Are you sure?"

She nodded. "I might be off by a few minutes, but no more than that."

"The neighbor said she heard the argument at quarter of twelve. She remembers because she was taking her daughter upstairs to put her down for her nap. The problem is, she says the argument was still going on when she came back down a half hour later."

Amanda shook her head. "That can't be. I know I wasn't there after twelve. If anything, I left a few minutes before that."

He was silent for a moment. "The autopsy report indicated that your father died from head injuries. It appears he was hit with a heavy object. He fell and hit his head on the fireplace hearth, fracturing his skull. The fractured skull has been determined to be the actual cause of death."

"Then it was an accident?"

He shook his head. "Unfortunately, if the first blow to his head caused him to fall, the person who delivered that blow would be held responsible for his death."

"You say that like you think I'm that person."

"The neighbor also said she saw a woman leave the house shortly after the argument ended."

Amanda folded her arms across her waist. She felt ill. "It wasn't me," she insisted, shaking her head. "I told you, I threw the ashtray, but I missed. He was fine when I left."

Drew put his arm around her shoulder. She looked at him. "He doesn't believe me." She turned her gaze on Claude. "Do you?"

Claude reached over and took her hand. "I believe you, Amanda, but that's not what matters."

"Will they arrest me?"

"They'll probably want to talk to you again."

"You mean question me. What do you recommend I do about that?"

"I recommend you talk to them. It would make you look more suspect if you refuse. I'll be with you when you talk to them."

On Friday, Drew arrived home to find Amanda immersed in the papers she had brought from her father's home. Drew had insisted they pack everything up and take it home. Aside from her father's house being the site of his recent death, the environment was simply too depressing for her to be expected to concentrate on business affairs.

She was seated on the floor of the den, surrounded by several piles of papers. She was so engrossed in her work, she had not heard him enter. He leaned over and placed a kiss on the top of her head.

"Hi, babe."

She swung around to face him. "Drew! What time is it? I've been so busy trying to get these papers in order, the time got away from me."

"I take it that means there's no dinner in the oven?"

Amanda opened her mouth to retort until she looked up and saw the grin on his face. "I'm afraid I can't even offer you a frozen dinner."

"So what'll it be, pizza or Chinese?"

"Either one."

Drew left her to her work and went to order dinner. After changing his clothes, he returned to the den.

"Have you been able to make any sense of it?"

"I've been going through the checkbook and the cancelled checks, trying to put them with the corresponding bills. All things considered, I'm surprised to see that it appears the bills are all current. I can't really be sure because it looks like some of the bills were discarded once they'd been paid."

"Have you been at this all day?"

"Pretty much. I found an insurance policy and from what I can determine from his checkbook, the premiums have been paid up to date. It's not much, but it'll cover the expenses. I called the company and the agent is supposed to call me back tomorrow."

She held up one of the documents. "I even found the deed to the house buried in all these papers, for whatever good that will do. I haven't found a will and I don't expect he wrote one."

Drew sat down on the floor beside her, looking through the papers she had already organized. It had been quite a task sorting through the boxes of haphazardly stored papers they had retrieved from her father's house.

Amanda was still at work when the doorbell rang. Drew went to answer it, returning a few minutes later.

"I think it's time for a break, sweetheart. Dinner has arrived."

"Okay, in a minute."

Amanda shrieked in surprise when Drew reached down, slid his hands under her and lifted her to her feet. "That can wait. You probably haven't eaten anything since breakfast, have you?"

"Not true. I had a banana and some coffee this afternoon."

"That's what I thought. Let's go."

He took her by the hand and led her to the kitchen. She washed her hands at the sink while he set the table. When she joined him, there was an array of Chinese food cartons spread out on the table.

"Are we having company?"

Drew smiled. "I couldn't make up my mind and I wasn't sure what you wanted."

For the next forty-five minutes, checkbooks, bills, and insurance were forgotten. The only discussion involved whether or not Amanda should try the extra-spicy chicken.

When they finished eating and the leftovers had been put away, Amanda returned to the den. She began clipping the checks together with whatever corresponding bills she could find. She had just finished that task and was starting to go through another stack of papers when Drew entered the room.

"Okay, babe, how about calling it a night?"

Amanda sighed. "I was hoping to finish these piles tonight, but I guess you're right."

She began picking papers up off the floor. Drew helped her stack them on the coffee table and they left the room. When they reached the bedroom, Amanda raised her eyebrow at the strange glow visible through the slightly open bathroom door. She walked over and pushed it open.

Drew was close behind. "I thought you might be in need of a nice relaxing bubble bath."

Amanda was in a daze, looking around at the

lighted candles and mounds of fragrant bubbles in the tub. It was just another example of the thoughtfulness of this wonderful man she had married.

Drew was behind her. She was still lost in thought when he pulled her shirt up over her head. He eased her slacks down her legs. She stepped out of them and he laid them aside with her shirt. He smiled when she trembled slightly as his hands unhooked her bra and sent it tumbling to the floor.

Amanda's trembling increased when he knelt down behind her, slipping his fingers in the waistband of her panties. She gasped, wishing for something to hold onto. Her knees shook when he slowly eased the panties down her legs, his fingers brushing her silky skin. He was so close, she could feel his breath on the backs of her thighs.

When he had finished his slow torture, he stood up. He lifted her in his arms and held her for a moment, savoring the feel of her silky skin. When she looked up at him, he lowered his mouth to capture hers in a long, searching kiss.

Amanda reached up to clutch his shoulder. Her heartbeat increased with the friction from the texture of his shirt against her bare breasts. She sighed when he broke the kiss.

"I think we'd better get you into the tub before the water gets cold."

He carried her the few steps to the tub and lowered her into the warm suds. When she was seated, he knelt at the side of the tub, took the sponge in hand, and began smoothing the lather over her body. Amanda closed her eyes and gave herself up to the foamy caresses.

All too soon, he was lifting her from the tub. She barely had time to recover before he had toweled her dry and was carrying her to the bed. He had turned

down the covers earlier and now he laid her on the
cool sheets, turning her over on her stomach. He
began slowly massaging the muscles that had been
tensed for weeks.

It felt so good, so soothing. Amanda tried to stay
awake. His earlier caresses had aroused her, but the
massage was having the opposite effect.

A few minutes later, Drew called her name. Receiving no response, he leaned across her body to see
her face. Her eyes were closed, but the real clue was
her soft, even breathing. She was sound asleep.

Drew pulled the covers up over her. He went to
retrieve her clothes and douse the candles. A few
minutes later, he undressed and slid into bed beside
her. Before long, he too was asleep, with her wrapped
in his arms.

Amanda awakened slowly the next morning still in
a fog. She opened her eyes and frowned, trying to
remember the previous evening. She remembered
Drew surprising her with a soothing bubble bath. She
also remembered what that bath had entailed. Finally, she recalled with embarrassment that she had
fallen asleep while he was giving her a massage. She
had no doubt that that was not the ending he had
anticipated for the evening.

She turned over in his arms and looked up at his
face. He was still asleep. Her hand began caressing
the warm brown skin, moving across his chest and
slowing down to play in the mat of hair. As her hand
traveled lower, she sprinkled kisses on his face and
then his chest. He groaned when her hand reached
the tangle of hair surrounding his now aroused manhood.

He opened his eyes and grinned. "Good morning."

Amanda's fingers continued their work. "Yes, it is, isn't it?"

Drew reached over and pulled her on top of him. Their lips met with all the unspent passion of the previous night. Drew's hands cupped her buttocks, and then eased lower to spread her thighs. Urging her knees forward, he entered her. Moving slowly at first, their rhythm soon became frenzied as they reached for ecstasy.

"Please, Drew."

Her plea for completion was barely a whisper. He turned so that their positions were reversed. His thrusts came harder and faster. Within moments, he felt her body tighten around him and they reached the pinnacle of ecstasy they had shared so many times before.

They lay there for a long time, savoring the closeness. Finally, Amanda stirred and sighed.

"As much as I'd like to stay right here for the rest of the day, I need to get back to work."

"I'll help you. Maybe we can finish this up today."

With the two of them working together, they had gone through all of the papers by lunchtime. Amanda found nothing else of importance and simply bundled up the papers and put them back in the box.

Twenty-one

Amanda had her interview with the police the following Monday afternoon. She had returned to work that morning. The weekend had been a pleasant interlude from the stress of the previous weeks. After laying her father to rest and achieving some order out of the chaos of his financial affairs, she had gained some peace of mind.

It was at this interview with the police that she learned that one of their main pieces of evidence was her fingerprints on the lamp. She told them she had probably touched the lamp while she was there. She did not mention that she had picked it up to hit her father and then changed her mind.

There were a few questions that Claude refused to allow her to answer. Claude dismissed their reference to her estrangement from her father.

"Obviously, your source is unaware that my client and her father had recently reconciled."

Amanda almost choked on that statement. It was true that the estrangement had ended, but one could hardly say they had reconciled.

The police thanked her for her cooperation. Amanda wished she could feel relieved, but she knew it was not ended. The investigation would continue.

* * *

On Tuesday evening, Evelyn called. "I haven't heard from you in a while. How are you?"

"Actually, I've been better. Quite a lot has happened since I last saw you."

Amanda told her about her confrontation with her father and his death. "It's a little scary. I still keep expecting the police to show up on my doorstep with a warrant for my arrest."

Evelyn was grateful that she was having this conversation over the telephone. It would have been difficult to hide her reaction if they were face-to-face. She let Amanda talk for a while, venting her fear and frustration.

"Amanda, surely they can't actually believe you'd do such a thing?"

"I'm not sure what they believe."

"Well, try not to worry, dear. I'm sure everything will be alright."

On Thursday afternoon, Drew was in the middle of a meeting with a client when his secretary buzzed him. "Yes, Betty, what is it?"

"There's a Mrs. Reed on the line."

"Did you tell her I'm in the middle of a meeting?"

"Yes, but she says it's important that she speak to you."

"Get her number and tell her I'll have to call her back." Fifteen minutes later, Drew dialed Evelyn's number. What could Evelyn Reed possibly want with him? It occurred to him that it might be business, but her statement that it was important had alerted him to the unlikelihood of that.

After they had dispensed with the usual greetings,

she hesitated. "Mrs. Reed, my secretary indicated there was some urgency in your call."

"Yes, I need to see you and Amanda. I have some important information concerning her father's death. I would have called sooner, but I knew nothing about the situation until I spoke with Amanda on Tuesday."

"This all sounds very cryptic. Why didn't you tell Amanda when you talked to her on the phone?"

"Because she might be upset when I tell her what I have to say. I think it would be best if you were with her."

Drew was a little impatient with the other woman's evasion, but he restrained himself from asking any further questions. He could see that he was not likely to get any further information from her on the phone.

"When would you like to speak with us?"

"Would this evening be convenient? I'd like to get this over with as soon as possible."

"This evening is fine. Would you like to come to dinner?"

She hesitated. "No, I think it would be better if I come after dinner."

He suggested seven-thirty. She agreed and they ended the conversation. After he hung up, Drew sat there for a long time, wondering what she could possibly have to tell them about James Reynolds's death. He was unaware that she had even known Amanda's father. In spite of the other information Amanda had withheld, he was sure she was ignorant of any connection between Evelyn Reed and her father.

Evelyn Reed was prompt. Drew had told Amanda of her impending visit and their strange conversation. They both met her at the door and ushered her into the living room.

"Can I get you anything? Coffee? Tea?"

"No, thank you, dear."

When she was settled, Evelyn cleared her throat. "I'm sure you're wondering why I'm here. When I tell you, you may be angry with me. As I explained on the phone, I didn't know what's been going on until I talked to Amanda on Tuesday. When she told me all that's happened and that the police suspect her, I had to come and talk to you."

"Drew said you hinted that you know something about my father's death."

She took a deep breath and clasped her hands in her lap, to keep them from shaking. "That's right. I think I may be the person who's responsible for James Reynolds's death. It wasn't intentional. I had no idea that when I hit him it would cause his death."

"You hit him? But why were you there? You never told me you knew him."

"Before I get into that, I want to tell you exactly what happened."

Drew held Amanda's hand as Evelyn explained her visit to Amanda's father and his threatening actions. He recalled that James Reynolds was an intimidating bully under normal conditions. It was easy to imagine the fear he could inspire bolstered by alcohol.

"You still haven't told us why you were there."

"I went to see your father to try to convince him to tell you the truth, or at least to stop playing on your sympathy. I've known your father for years. I knew your mother, too. She was very special to me."

She blinked back the tears. "The truth is, your mother is the patient I'd been visiting for years at the nursing home. I didn't tell you before because you already had enough to cope with when you discovered she was alive."

"If you knew my parents, then you must have known me, too."

"Yes, but I had no idea where your father had taken you when you moved away. I hadn't seen you since you were three years old."

Drew watched Amanda closely. The mere fact that Evelyn had known Amanda as a child and had deliberately kept that knowledge from her was puzzling.

"Amanda, the truth that I tried to convince your father to reveal is that he was not your biological father. Your mother was pregnant with you when he married her."

Amanda's eyes widened. She frowned. "Why are you telling me this? What difference does that make now? And what business is it of yours?"

"It's my business because I'm your grandmother. Your biological father was my son. He was killed in a car accident before you were born."

She sighed. "I know this is a lot to take in. I don't blame you if you're angry with me. If you'd like me to leave, I'll understand."

Amanda hesitated. Evelyn stood up. She took a few steps toward the hall, but Amanda stopped her.

"No, don't leave. I think I need to hear this."

Evelyn returned to her seat. "Are you sure?"

"Yes, I think it's time I knew the whole truth."

Evelyn nodded. "Your mother and father were only seventeen years old when she became pregnant. My son, Michael, told me as soon as he knew. Elizabeth was terrified of telling her parents. Michael arranged to meet her at her home. He was determined to marry her and they planned to tell her parents together."

She took a deep breath and wiped away a few tears. "Elizabeth called my home when Michael was an hour late arriving. Less than half an hour after her call, the police were at my door, telling me that Michael had been killed in a car accident. A drunk driver ran a red light and smashed into the driver's side of the car.

"Eventually, Elizabeth and I had an opportunity to talk. I tried to persuade her to come and live with me, that she could finish school, even go on to college. I'd help her raise the child.

"She told me she was seriously considering marrying James Reynolds. I tried to talk her out of it. I knew something about him from what Michael had told me."

She looked at Amanda, blinking back the tears. "Your mother was a beautiful young woman. James Reynolds had been obsessed with her for years. He had convinced her that he loved her and that the fact that she was carrying another man's child didn't matter."

"What about her parents? Didn't they try to help?"

"Oh, they helped, alright. They helped convince her that marrying James was the right thing to do."

"So she married him."

"I suppose the relationship was alright for a while. We kept in touch and after you were born, Elizabeth would bring you to visit me."

"Nonnie," Amanda whispered.

Evelyn smiled. "You remember?"

"We used to have tea parties."

"Yes, your mother would leave you with me while she went shopping. You loved those tea parties. You were such an adorable child."

Amanda shook her head. "I can't remember much more. Why did we stop visiting you?"

"James became angry about the time your mother was spending with me. She tried to explain that she was busy with other errands many of the times you were with me. She told me he insisted they couldn't be a real family as long as she continued to cling to Michael's mother."

Amanda closed her eyes. Her voice was little more than a whisper. "He wasn't nice to her."

"What do you mean, Amanda?" Evelyn asked softly.

"He used to yell at her, a lot."

She looked up at Evelyn. "What really happened to my mother? Dr. Ormond said she had a mental breakdown after her baby died. Do you know what really happened?"

"Not exactly. I know she was miserable the entire time. In spite of the fact that James had tried to eliminate all contact with me, she used to call me sometimes. The poor child had no one else. She told me he accused her of having an affair. He said he didn't believe the second baby was his."

She shook her head. "Losing that child was just too much for her to bear."

"But she had me. How could she just leave me like that?"

Drew put his arm around her. He could understand how abandoned she must have felt, still felt.

"She didn't abandon you, child. I suppose somewhere in her confused mind she knew you would be taken care of, if not by James, by me. The truth is, I think her mind had been going for some time. When the baby was stillborn, the shock was too much. It just pushed her over the edge."

Amanda said nothing. She was trying to understand what her mother must have suffered. She knew firsthand what her father was like, his constant faultfinding and accusations. She remembered his statement that she was not like her mother, that her mother was weak.

"Amanda, honey, your mother loved you more than anything or anyone in this world."

She nodded, her attention still focused on her hands. She knew Evelyn was telling the truth. She remembered being sung to and held and loved. "I know."

She looked at Evelyn. "I can't say the same for him. I don't think he ever loved me. At least now I understand why. What I don't understand is why he bothered to take me with him."

"I'm not sure of James Reynolds's motivation for anything, but I have a couple of ideas. He knew I would take you in a minute. He disliked me so much, he'd have done anything to prevent that. The overriding reason was probably the fact that he could get Social Security benefits for you."

As she watched her granddaughter's reaction, Evelyn wondered if it had been wise to come. "I'm sorry to hit you with this all at once, but I didn't want you to find out the truth from someone else. The whole story will have to come out when I go to the police. James's death took the choice of timing out of my hands."

"I'm still not sure why he would threaten you."

"I guess he knew that if I told you the truth, you would begin to see him for what he really was. There would be no more opportunity for him to try to wheedle money out of you."

Drew had been watching Amanda and her reaction. Now he looked up sharply at Evelyn. Then he turned back to Amanda.

"You gave him money?"

Amanda looked down at her hands. She should have known that bit of information was bound to come out.

"Just a few dollars. He said his job had let him go

when he had the car accident. When it occurred to me that he should be eligible for unemployment benefits, I needed to ask him about it. That's why I went there that day, to ask him about it. That's what started the argument."

Evelyn looked at Drew. "I know the idea of Amanda giving James money is upsetting to you and I guess it's none of my business. You might call me a meddlesome old woman, but don't be too disappointed in Amanda. I'm sure you know by now that you're married to a kindhearted woman who's sometimes generous to a fault."

Before he could reply, Amanda answered for him. "Drew would never call you meddlesome. And he's always been very patient with me, even though I'm sure that patience has been stretched almost to the breaking point more than once."

Drew hugged his wife. He was not totally surprised at Evelyn's revelation.

"Amanda's right. I know you're only concerned about her welfare."

"I must admit that seeing you two together has done me a world of good. I worried about you for years. When James disappeared with you, I had no idea where he'd gone. When I saw you sitting there in the lobby at the nursing home, it was an answer to my prayer."

"You knew who I was right away? You didn't even know who I was visiting. It's hard to believe you could recognize me from your memory of a toddler."

Evelyn opened her purse and pulled out a photograph of a handsome young man. Even Amanda immediately recognized the resemblance to herself.

"That's Michael, your father." Amanda fingered the photograph thoughtfully. Her father. How different her life might have been if not for the criminal negligence of a drunk driver. On the other hand, if she had been raised by two happily married parents, she might never have met Drew. She handed the photo back to Evelyn.

Evelyn placed it back in her purse and stood up. "I'd better be going. I have a big day ahead of me tomorrow. I wanted you to know the whole story before I go to the police."

Amanda's heart thumped. She had forgotten the event that had prompted this visit.

"You can't go alone. And you certainly can't go without an attorney.

Drew spoke up. "She's right. Why don't you stay here tonight? In the morning I'll call an attorney friend of mine."

Evelyn looked uncertain. "I don't know. I think I've prevailed upon your patience enough."

Drew stood up and walked over to her. "You're part of the family now. As part of the family, we have to do whatever we can to help."

He cast a glance at his wife. "Amanda would never forgive me, and I'd never forgive myself if we let you just walk out of our lives."

Evelyn shook her head. "I didn't come here for that. I don't want to take advantage of your kindness."

She looked down at her hands. She was a proud woman and she had been alone, taking care of herself, for many years.

"That would make me no better than James Reynolds."

Amanda jumped up from her seat and came over to her. She hugged her, taking Evelyn by surprise. When Amanda pulled back, they both had tears in their eyes.

"Don't ever put yourself in the same category as

him. You got into this situation trying to look out for me. You were forced out of my life more than twenty years ago. Please, don't walk out of my life again."

Evelyn reached out, wiping the tears from Amanda's eyes. "I'd never do that, honey. I just don't want either of you to feel responsible for helping me get out of this mess."

"It's our mess now. We'll handle it together."

With some urging, she led the older woman up the stairs to the guest room. The two of them worked together making the bed. Amanda reminisced about the few memories she had of her early childhood, the happier parts.

"I'll go find something for you to sleep in," Amanda said when they finished making the bed.

She smiled when she thought about her usual sleeping attire. She could imagine her grandmother's face if she took her one of the sheer nighties she had received at her shower. Fortunately, she had not discarded her other nightgowns and pajamas.

Amanda returned a few minutes later holding a long, full cotton gown in one hand and a pile of bath linens in the other. "This should fit," she suggested.

She laid the linens on the bed. "The bathroom is next door," she explained gesturing to the right. She hesitated. "Try not to worry. Mr. Oglethorpe is a very good attorney."

"Thank you, Amanda. I'm not worried. God's been with me all these years. He'll help me through this, too."

Amanda kissed her cheek. "Good night, Nonnie."

"Good night, baby."

Twenty-two

On Friday morning, Amanda was making breakfast when Evelyn entered the kitchen. "Good morning. Did you sleep alright?"

"Fine, dear. Can I help with anything?"

"No, thanks. Have a seat. Would you like some coffee? Or would you prefer tea?"

"Coffee is fine, thank you."

Amanda set the mug of coffee on the table just as Drew entered the kitchen. He came over to Amanda, put his arm around her waist, and kissed her cheek.

"Good morning, again."

The heat crept up Amanda's neck when she remembered his first "good morning" an hour earlier, and what had followed that greeting. "Morning, Drew," she murmured.

Evelyn smiled and focused her attention on her coffee. Drew joined her at the table after pouring himself a mug of coffee.

"I'm not sure what time Claude will be able to see you today. I'll give him a call at home in a little while. I don't have any urgent appointments at the office, so I'll wait here until I contact him."

"Call me at work when you have an appointment time. I'd like to be there."

"I have a better idea. Why don't you call me when

you get to work and let me know what would be a good time for you. I'm sure I can get Claude to work around that, even if it means seeing us after regular office hours."

The appointment with Claude was scheduled for four o'clock. Drew and Evelyn arrived first and Claude was brought up-to-date on the latest development in the death of James Reynolds.

"Did he injure you?"

"Not really. He grabbed me, but when I stumbled, it loosened his hold on me and I backed away. When he came after me again, my hand touched the lamp. I grabbed it without thinking and swung at him. I surprised myself when I actually hit him. He stumbled back and I got out of there. I didn't think I'd really hurt him. In fact, the whole time I was hurrying to my car I kept looking back to see if he was coming after me."

"What time did you arrive?"

"I'd guess it must have been a little after twelve. I'm judging that from the time I left home. It had to have been after twelve o'clock."

Claude nodded. Amanda arrived at that moment. He repeated Evelyn's statement.

"That explains the neighbor's statement. What she heard was two separate arguments, not a continuation of the same argument."

He informed Evelyn of the statement given by the next-door neighbor. He also gave her the information from the autopsy report.

"So where do we go from here?"

"We have a choice to make. Or rather, you have a choice. One option is to do nothing. The police may drop the matter and simply rule the death accidental."

"Or?"

"Or they may charge Amanda with manslaughter. I think that would be the strongest charge they could make. If that happens, you could then make another decision whether or not to come forth."

"You mean let Amanda go to trial?"

"Yes."

Evelyn shook her head. "That's not an option."

Claude explained what Evelyn could expect when she made her statement to the police. It was decided that she would wait until Monday to go to the police.

"I think before you plan to accompany me to the police station, I need to know more about your fee."

Claude smiled. "Why don't we worry about that after we see if you'll even be needing my services?"

"What about this consultation?"

"If I have to represent you for any further action, the consultation will be included in that fee."

Evelyn had the feeling she was being given the runaround. Since it was a very nice runaround, she did not press the issue.

When they left Claude's office, they stopped at a small restaurant for an early dinner. Amanda tried to get Evelyn to stay with them for the weekend, but she refused. She cited the fact that she had no extra clothes. Amanda suggested she drive her home, wait while she packed a bag, and drive her back to spend the next two days in Philadelphia.

Evelyn insisted she needed to return to her own home. She refrained from mentioning the possibility that once she made her statement to the police, she might be placed under arrest. She had to prepare for that eventuality.

* * *

On Monday morning Evelyn, accompanied by Claude, had her interview with the police. When Sergeant Lafferty read her her rights, she had a moment of fear, but calmed herself. She explained her visit to James Reynolds and the events that transpired during that visit. They asked a few questions, which she answered honestly. Although she knew she was not in the clear yet, she was relieved when they thanked her and let her go.

"So, what happens now?" she asked Claude as they left the police station.

"They'll continue investigating. They'll check up on you, your background, your credibility. I'll be arranging for some investigating of my own. You said James Reynolds's attitude was threatening. I plan to find out more about him, if he had ever been violent before."

He drove her back to his office. "Would you like to come in and call Amanda?"

She shook her head. "I don't think so. You can tell her what happened at the interview. Just tell her I'll call her tomorrow."

She shook his hand. "I appreciate your help. Thank you for everything, Mr. Oglethorpe."

"You're quite welcome, Mrs. Reed. Let's hope this is the only time you'll need my services. I'll keep in touch."

True to his word, Claude investigated James Reynolds. What he learned was that there had been several altercations with the victim's neighbors in the previous year. Most of them centered around the condition of his property, which was why they had decided to go to him as a group.

He also learned that he had been fired from his job as a bailiff a few years earlier as a result of several near-violent arguments with coworkers. He had been given an opportunity to seek treatment for his drinking problem and had refused, denying he had a problem.

The police had discovered much the same information in their investigation. When Sergeant Lafferty took his information to the captain, it was decided that there was no point in taking the case to the district attorney. The likelihood of receiving any conviction against the kindly grandmother who had defended herself against an enraged alcoholic was very slim, at best.

Thursday afternoon, Claude received a telephone call from Sergeant Lafferty, informing him that their would be no charges filed against either of his clients. It had been determined that Mrs. Reed had acted in self-defense and James Reynolds's death was ruled accidental.

He immediately called Evelyn and gave her the good news. There was a moment of silence after he delivered the message.

"Mrs. Reed, are you there?"

"Yes, yes, I'm here. Thank you, Mr. Oglethorpe."

"You're welcome. Would you like for me to call Drew and Amanda?"

"No, thank you. I'll call them this evening."

"Well, I'm glad it ended this way. Take care of yourself, Mrs. Reed." He started to hang up, but she called his name.

"Mr. Oglethorpe, you still haven't told me what I owe you. Will you send me the bill?"

"Mrs. Reed, I really didn't do anything."

"I think you did and I expect to receive a bill for the consultation, just like any other client."

"Very well, Mrs. Reed, I'll send you a bill for the consultation."

Claude sighed and hung up the telephone. He

knew a few other women like Evelyn Reed—proud,
black women. He could simply forget to send a bill,
but he knew that would not be the end of it.

That evening, Amanda and Drew had just finished
dinner and settled in the den when Evelyn called.
Amanda answered the telephone. When Evelyn gave
her the news, she could not keep the tears from
springing to her eyes.

"That's wonderful, Nonnie. I'm so glad."

They talked for a long time. Before they hung up,
Evelyn promised to come for a longer visit the following weekend. She turned to Drew, who was seated
beside her.

"I guess I can assume the police have dropped the
charges?"

She nodded. "It's all over. They've ruled my father's death accidental. Nonnie said Mr. Oglethorpe
called her this afternoon."

Drew took her in his arms, pulling her onto his
lap. "Maybe now you'll finally relax. I know you've
been carrying a heavy load for months."

Amanda entwined her arms around his neck.
"You've made it a lot easier, Drew. In spite of the fact
that I've put you through a lot, too."

"Have you forgotten what I keep telling you?"

Amanda smiled. "No, I haven't forgotten. 'That's
what husbands are for,' right?"

"Right."

"I think we decided wives are for pretty much the
same thing, right?"

"That's right."

Drew's hand crept up her skirt, stroking her thigh.
He nuzzled her neck as his lips traced kisses along
her shoulder.

"Of course, there are other things a wife is for."

"I'd say that pretty much works both ways, too."

The next hour was spent demonstrating some of the very pleasant functions of husbands and wives. It was an especially sweet celebration, signalling the end of the secrets that had briefly threatened their happiness and their love.

Epilogue

Drew entered the den to see Amanda staring at the paper in her hand. She was sitting sideways on the sofa, her knees bent with a notebook resting on them. It was probably the first few minutes of relaxation she had had all day, but she did not seem happy about it.

"That didn't take long," she murmured, her eyes still on the notebook. "Are they asleep?"

"They were asleep before I finished two pages of the story."

"You realize some people think we're strange, reading stories to babies not even two months old."

He walked over and sat down on the other end of the sofa. "I hope that frown isn't because people think we're strange, sweetheart?"

"I've been going over this list for the party after the twins' dedication. Every time I look at it, I realize there's someone else that should be included."

"How many do you have on the list now?"

"Thirty-five."

"That's not so bad. We have plenty of room. We should be able to entertain that number comfortably."

"The problem is preparing the food for all those people."

Drew chuckled. She looked up, frowning. "You find this amusing?"

"I was just thinking. If we had planned this better, we'd have had the twins in the spring and we could have had a barbecue outdoors."

Amanda cleared her throat. "As I recall, there wasn't much planning involved, other than the decision that we were ready to have children. If a certain man I know had shown a little more restraint, the results of that decision might have taken a little longer to bear fruit, no pun intended."

Drew laughed out loud at that statement. He sat back against the cushions and pulled her legs straight across his lap. He began caressing her legs. "If a certain woman didn't go around looking so sexy, a certain man might be able to show restraint."

Amanda took a deep breath when his fingers reached the backs of her knees. "You're not helping matters, Drew."

"I have the solution. Hire a caterer."

"A caterer? That's too expensive."

"Have you checked it out?"

"Well . . . no, but caterers aren't cheap."

"I hired a caterer for the Christmas party. If you recall, it was really quite reasonable."

Amanda hesitated.

He reached over and took her face in his hands. "We can afford it, Amanda. It will be worth it to me, knowing you're not running yourself crazy trying to prepare for the party. You have enough to keep you busy already."

"Are you sure about this, Drew?"

"I'm sure." He lowered his hands. His arms encircled her waist and moments later she was sitting on his lap.

"Now that that's settled, we can move on to more important matters."

"Drew, would you zip me up, please?" She walked across the room and presented her back to him.

Her husband obliged her and placed his usual kiss at the nape of her neck. It had become a habit with him. He had done it scores of times and each time it gave Amanda a little shiver of anticipation.

She returned to the dressing table. After applying her lipstick, she slipped her feet into the gray suede pumps that complemented the burgundy wool A-line dress with the softly draped cowl neck.

"Is the diaper bag packed?"

"All but the bottles."

Amanda looked over from her task of filling the gray suede clutch bag. "Are you ready?"

"All set," he assured her, looking at the two bundles lying on the huge bed surrounded by pillows. The two babies were quite content, sucking on their pacifiers.

"I'll go start the car and come back to help. I'll take the diaper bag with me and pack the bottles."

He returned a few minutes later. After bundling up the babies, they were on their way to the church.

The babies were amazingly quiet during the service. Toward the end of the service, Reverend Walters began the dedication service.

"I have one more pleasant duty today. Would the Connors family join me at the altar, please?"

Amanda and Drew stood up, each holding a child. They made their way to the front of the church where they were joined by Drew's parents, Evelyn, and Jennifer on one side. On the other side stood Nicole and David, the twins' godparents.

"Friends, I take great pleasure in introducing to you Elizabeth Claire Connors and Michael Andrew Connors, two of God's most recent miracles."

Reverend Walters proceeded, charging the parents and godparents with their responsibilities. When the ceremony was over and the babies had been blessed, Amanda and Drew returned to their seats.

A few minutes later, Amanda glanced at Claire, when the minister's morning sermon touched on the importance of families. She remembered the day the breach had been healed between Drew's mother and herself.

After the fiasco at the older woman's birthday party, Amanda noticed that the snide remarks and insults stopped. After that Claire was not exactly friendly, but she was no longer hostile.

Their differences had disappeared entirely when Amanda went into labor three weeks early, in the middle of Jennifer's wedding shower. Nicole was prepared to drive her to the hospital, but she had never expected Claire to insist on accompanying them.

Drew was out of town on business, scheduled to return that evening. Claire sat in the back seat with her on the ride to the hospital. She stayed with her the entire time until Drew's arrival.

It was later, when she was no longer caught in the pain of giving birth, that Amanda recalled the soothing presence of her mother-in-law. It was Claire who insisted that Amanda hold onto her hand in the car and squeeze when the pain hit. It was Claire who stayed by her side in those early stages of labor, coaching her and wiping her forehead.

* * *

An hour later, the family was assembled at Drew and Amanda's home to celebrate. Aside from the family the guests included a few neighbors, Drew's employees, and Amanda's coworkers. Amanda had not expected the event to turn into such a large party. She had followed Drew's suggestion and hired a caterer, which was not nearly as expensive as she had originally anticipated.

After she had made the arrangements, Kenneth and Claire had offered to take care of the expense. When she balked at that offer, Claire took her aside.

"I wish you would let us do this, Amanda. It's my fault we never bought a wedding gift for you. I'd feel much better if you'd allow us to make this small gesture."

Hearing Claire asking for permission as if she considered it a privilege was the deciding factor for Amanda. "This isn't necessary, Claire, but if you really want to do it, that's fine with me. Thank you."

Halfway through the party, someone suggested a photograph of the entire family. Nicole offered to be the photographer. She directed each member to the place she considered appropriate. Kenneth and Drew found themselves being ushered to stand behind their respective mates.

As they made their way to the sofa in the living room, Kenneth leaned over and murmured to Drew, "That's a sight I had almost despaired of ever seeing."

"What's that, Dad?"

He gestured toward Amanda and Claire sitting side by side on the sofa. "Our wives not only getting along, but actually smiling and talking."

"I know what you mean, Dad. I guess the fact that

Amanda's the mother of her first grandchildren makes a difference. Amanda told me how she stayed with her during the labor."

Kenneth shook his head. "That may be part of it, son, but it's only a very small part. I think they've both learned a lesson about keeping secrets from the people who love them."

Drew glanced at him. "I think there's something more that you're not telling me."

"That's right, son," was all Kenneth would say. The discussion between Claire and himself was very private and personal.

"I take it you have no intention of telling me."

Kenneth smiled. "Right again."

Drew chuckled. "Well, it doesn't matter what brought about the change. I have no doubt we can all overcome any differences we may have in the future."

Kenneth put his arm around his son's shoulder. "That's what's important. That's what families are all about."

Dear Readers,

I hope you enjoyed this story of a loving, but unexpected reunion. Unlike my last novel, *False Impressions,* I kept the setting closer to home, in Philadelphia, PA.

Secrets of the Heart, like *False Impressions,* contains a plot that involves more than the usual relationship problems. Although, it contains some of those problems, too.

Thanks to all of you who have written or e-mailed me to let me know you enjoy my novels. I hope you will continue to enjoy them.

Please continue to write. I appreciate your opinions and, to date, I have succeeded in my efforts to reply to each message.

> Yours truly,
> Marilyn Tyner
> P.O. Box 219
> Yardley, PA 19067
> E-mail address: mtyner1@juno.com

ABOUT THE AUTHOR

Marilyn Tyner has published several African American romance novels in the past three years. Ms. Tyner grew up in a small town outside of Pittsburgh and currently resides in another small town outside of Philadelphia.

In addition to writing, she is a caseworker for the Pennsylvania Department of Public Welfare. Her busy schedule includes being an active member of the Order of Cyrene, PHA and the Order of the Eastern Star, PHA.

She is the mother of two adult children and has three grandchildren.